true colors

true colors

natalie kinsey-warnock

alfred a. knopf   new york

THIS IS A BORZOI BOOK PUBLISHED BY ALFRED A. KNOPF

All rights reserved. Published in the United States by Alfred A. Knopf, an imprint of Random House Children's Books, a division of Random House, Inc., New York.

Knopf, Borzoi Books, and the colophon are registered trademarks of Random House, Inc.

Visit us on the Web! randomhouse.com/kids

Educators and librarians, for a variety of teaching tools, visit us at RHTeachersLibrarians.com

Library of Congress Cataloging-in-Publication Data
Kinsey-Warnock, Natalie.
True colors / by Natalie Kinsey-Warnock.
p. cm.
Summary: In 1952 Vermont, ten-year-old Blue decides to set out in the middle of her town's sesquicentennial celebration to find the mother who abandoned her as a baby, but a series of events reminds her that she already has everything she needs.
ISBN 978-0-375-86099-7 (trade) — ISBN 978-0-375-96099-4 (lib. bdg.) —
ISBN 978-0-375-89706-1 (ebook) — ISBN 978-0-375-85453-8 (tr. pbk.)
[1. Identity—Fiction. 2. Farm life—Vermont—Fiction. 3. Foundlings—Fiction.
4. People with mental disabilities—Fiction. 5. Vermont—History—20th century—
Fiction.] I. Title.
PZ7.K6293Tr 2012
[Fic]—dc23
2011037863

The text of this book is set in 11-point Century Book.

Printed in the United States of America
November 2012
10 9 8 7 6 5 4 3 2 1

First Edition

In loving memory of my sister, Helen,
for instilling in me a love of history and family stories.

- - ✕-✕✕ - - - - - - - - - - - - - -

For Lisa and Jana,
for letting me "borrow" their grandfather Wallace Gilpin
for this story.

- - - - - - - - - - - - - - ✕✕- - -

And in memory of Beverly Ross,
the real three-pound, two-day-old baby who
was found stuffed in a mailbox in 1926
and lived to tell the story.

true colors

chapter 1

June 1952

On a cold, clear December day in 1941, when I was but two days old, on the very same Sunday the Japanese bombed Pearl Harbor, I was found stuffed into the copper kettle Hannah Spooner grew her marigolds in. Even though I was wrapped in a tattered quilt, my skin was blue, bluer than a robin's egg, as blue as the tears I imagined in my mother's eyes when she left me there, with not even a note pinned to my diaper to give a clue as to who I was or where I'd come from.

Hannah carried me inside and warmed my cold, still body in her oven, just as she had newborn lambs, until I was pink again and squalling for my supper.

As news spread through town, folks nearly tripped over each other rushing out to Hannah's farm to see the Kettle Baby.

"Why, Hannah!" her friends said. "You're sixty-three

years old! You can't be raising up a child at your age." But Hannah had decided to keep me, and I love her like flowers love the sun, but still, bringing creatures home is Hannah's nature, so I figure I was just one more creature that needed nursing back to health. All these years, I've wondered what was wrong with me to cause my real mother to throw me away as if I were nothing more than a banana peel or a day-old newspaper.

So when I saw the cat near Hannah's barn, wild-eyed and skinny as a rake handle, and Hannah said it'd likely been left behind last year by one of the summer people when they headed back to the city, I felt my heart snag like cloth on a blackberry bramble.

"I know just how you feel," I told the cat.

I carried a bowl of milk out, but the cat took off across the pasture. I set the bowl down, anyway. She might come back.

Hannah didn't know it, but I had a secret. All these years, I've been waiting and watching for my mama to come back, too.

I looked down the road, as I did every day, but it was empty. She might not come today, or tomorrow, but some-day she'll show up, saying how she made a terrible mistake, that she didn't know what she was doing when she left me, that she really loves me and wants me back. I'll kiss Hannah goodbye, climb into my mama's brand-new 1952 DeSoto, and off we'll go to see the world.

Every once in a while, Hannah saves out enough of her egg money to take me to the movies (she especially loves Humphrey Bogart), and we share a root beer float at Pierce's Pharmacy, but my real mama will take me to the movies every day, and she'll buy me ice cream for breakfast, dinner, and supper if I want.

"Blue?" Hannah's voice carried out to me and chased the dreams from my head. "Are you feeding that cat out of my good china?"

You heard right. Hannah named me Blue—Blue Sky, to be exact—for my eyes and for being the same color, when she found me, as that clear December sky. Hannah says she thought long and hard about what to name me. I think she should have thought longer and harder, and come up with something better. I know hound dogs and cows with better names than I got, but I guess I'll have to live with it, at least until my real mama comes to claim me, and then I'll have a whole new name to go along with my new life.

chapter 2

Hannah's was the last farm near Shadow Lake. Even though it was a small farm—only seven cows, a couple of sheep, and some chickens—the summer people enjoyed coming by to help with the haying or to let their children ride Hannah's old white horse, Dolly.

"See this?" they'd tell the children as we forked hay onto the wagon or milked the cows by hand. "This is how things were done in the olden days."

Everything on the farm was old, but Hannah kept it all neat and tidy, and her flower garden was so beautiful no one noticed that the porch roof sagged or the barn needed paint.

The summer people may have thought it was fun to spend some of their vacation helping out, but for Hannah and me, summer was *work*. Besides doing the everyday chores of feeding the animals, milking the cows, cleaning gutters, spreading manure, and collecting eggs (which the hens always hid in at least a dozen different places), there was haying to be done. It could take all summer, and it was hot, itchy, backbreaking work. When it looked like there'd be at least three dry days in a row (and three dry days in a row in Vermont is about as common as a whistling pig, Hannah says), Hannah hitched up Dolly to the mower and mowed like crazy. After the sun dried the grass, we raked it so the sun could dry out the underside, too, then pitched the hay up onto a wagon, took it to the barn, and pitched all that hay off the wagon into the barn bays. We had to put up enough hay to feed the livestock through the whole winter (and winter in northern Vermont can last seven months).

Sometimes when summer people talked about how farming was so relaxing, I just wanted to shake 'em till their teeth rattled.

"Relaxing, my foot," Hannah would say.

One thing about all that work—I was strong. I could lift the full milk cans into Mr. Hazelton's truck when he came to pick them up every morning, and I could carry a hundred-pound bag of grain. Hannah was even stronger. She could lug *two* bags of grain, one under each arm.

"We're not women to be trifled with," Hannah says.

Then there was the gardening. Hannah had a huge garden that had to be tilled, planted, and weeded all summer long, because it fed us all winter, too.

When we weren't working, we went berrying. Picking

5

berries was Hannah's idea of fun, but to me, it just seemed like more work. Hannah and I picked pails of wild strawberries (it takes hours to pick a pail of tiny wild strawberries, and as much time to hull them, but even I had to admit there was nothing better-tasting than wild strawberries), wild raspberries, currants, gooseberries, and blueberries.

Besides milk and eggs, Hannah sold home-baked goods to the summer people, and I delivered them on Dolly. Those summer people couldn't get enough of Hannah's pies (made with all those berries we picked), bread, cakes, muffins, and her famous doughnuts. We would have been hard-pressed without that money, but every week, Hannah managed to save out a few dollars to put into a jar she'd labeled BLUE'S COLLEGE FUND.

Hannah was proud of that college fund, but it made me nervous. I didn't even like grade school—what made Hannah think I was going to like *college*? I hadn't decided yet whether I was going to run away and join a circus (I didn't like clowns, but I could see myself as a lion tamer) or go out west and be a cowboy. Either way, Hannah was in for a big disappointment.

It wasn't just the summer people who ordered Hannah's baked goods. She had dozens of regular customers, spread out over ten miles, and no matter how late it was, or how tired I was, or how much in a hurry I was, Mrs. Wells had to tell me about how her bunions were acting up, or how her daughter's baby was teething, or show me pictures of her ancestors who'd been dead about a thousand years. Every time I had a delivery for her, I wished I could just toss her order onto the porch as I was riding by, like a newspaper.

"She's lonely, poor thing," Hannah would say when I complained. "It won't hurt you to spend a few minutes listening to her."

The Trombley farm wasn't a short stop, either. Mr. Trombley had gotten his arm caught in a dragsaw and had spent two months in the hospital. Neighbors had pitched in to do his chores and haying, and all the women had been taking turns bringing in meals. Hannah sent a big basket every week, packed with enough food to feed a small army, which I guess the Trombleys were, seeing as how there were seven kids. Those kids were always climbing all over me, wanting to see what I'd brought, wanting me to play with them, and wanting to ride Dolly. It was hard to get away.

After the Trombley farm, my next deliveries were in town. As I rode past the fairgrounds, I saw banners saying SESQUICENTENNIAL! I wouldn't have understood what that meant except I knew this summer was the town's 150th anniversary. Four days of activities were being planned: a parade, a speech by the governor, pageants covering the town's history, horse pulling, harness racing, a bake sale, a supper in the town hall, and fireworks. It was going to happen August 13 to 16, and would be the biggest celebration this town had ever seen.

My last stop was the *Monitor* office. The *Monitor* was our weekly newspaper, and every Wednesday, I delivered three dozen doughnuts there. Wednesday night was when everyone at the office stayed up late making up the paper, which meant getting it ready to be printed, and even here, outside, I could hear the thump and clack of the printing press, which would be running all night. There was always so much excitement at the *Monitor* on printing nights that I wished I could stay up all night with them, but I knew Hannah wouldn't let me do that (Who'd help me with the chores in the morning? I could hear her saying), so I had to be content with watching them for a little while after I delivered the doughnuts. The editor, Mr. Wallace Gilpin, said he didn't think they could get the paper out without Hannah's doughnuts to keep them going. Mr. Gilpin always gave me a nickel, and I'd rush over to the five-and-ten-cent store before it closed and buy penny candy. I'd agonize over what to pick—root beer barrels, Tootsie Rolls, licorice sticks, horehound drops, bubble gum—then buy one of each, and they'd last most of the ride home.

Dolly stopped right at the *Monitor* door; she knew our route so well I often thought Dolly could make the deliveries all by herself (but then I wouldn't have gotten my nickel). I slid off her back, carried the bag of doughnuts up the steps, and was just reaching for the doorknob when the door burst open and Raleigh True charged out, barreling right over me.

chapter 3

The bag of doughnuts went flying. So did I, though Raleigh didn't even stop to see if I was all right, which wasn't like him. He disappeared around the side of the building, and then I heard shouting.

I should have run inside and gotten Mr. Gilpin, but Hannah's always saying I don't think before I act, and I guess she's right, because I ran after Raleigh instead.

Behind the *Monitor* office was where the river ran through town. At one time, it had been a busy place, with mills all up and down along the river, but most were now fallen in, with weeds growing in and around them. Teenagers liked to hang out in those old buildings, and they were littered with cigarette butts and broken beer bottles.

Waterfalls tumbled down the hillside, where, every spring, I liked to watch the steelheads leaping the falls, on their way upriver to spawn. Almost every day, I'd see Mr.

Hazelton fishing in the river, but he wasn't there today. Too bad, because he might have been able to stop what happened.

First thing I saw was Raleigh cradling a heron in his arms. The second thing I saw was Dennis and Wesley swaggering toward him, just like the showdown between Gary Cooper and the bad guys in *High Noon*, except Gary Cooper wasn't holding a heron.

"Hand it over, Frankenstein," Dennis said.

From a nest high in a tree, three baby herons hopped and squawked for their mother. All I could think was that Dennis and Wesley must have been throwing rocks and knocked the heron from its nest, and Raleigh must have seen them through the window.

Dennis and Wesley Wright were known throughout town as the Wright brothers, but they were as far from Orville and Wilbur as boys could get, I imagined. They'd started smoking and swearing when they were four, and were stealing and setting fires by the time they started school. They burned down Mr. Emerson's outhouse, tried to burn Mr. Hazelton's garage (his dog ran them off), and threw a firecracker into Mrs. Gauthier's chicken coop. Those poor hens were so traumatized they never laid eggs again and ended up in the soup pot. Since then, the Wright brothers had moved on to smashing mailboxes and windows, slashing tires, and stealing anything that wasn't chained down. The only thing I had in common with them was that they didn't have a mother, either. I remembered Hannah telling me once how Mrs. Wright had died giving birth to them, leaving Mr. Wright to raise the boys. Hannah had sighed and shaken her head.

"They would have been better off being raised by wolves," she'd said.

I thought she might be right, except the wolves probably would have been terrified of them, too. Dennis and Wesley were even meaner to animals than they were to other kids. They'd tied a firecracker to Dolly's tail and lit it, which might explain why Dolly was terrified of fireworks, and once in the horse shed at school, Dolly got stung over a hundred times after the Wright brothers peppered a hornets' nest with green apples, which might explain why Dolly was terrified of hornets *and* the Wright brothers. But of all the people and animals they terrorized, Raleigh was their favorite target.

Raleigh wasn't a kid—he was thirty-one years old (I knew that from counting the candles Hannah had put on the cake she'd made him for his last birthday), but he was "slow." He only spoke a few words, and it was hard to tell how much he understood of what other people said. Raleigh had a lopsided grin and a dent in his head, just above his ear, where the hair didn't grow. He did look a little like Frankenstein, though I would never have called him that.

Hannah said he'd had an accident ten years ago, but she didn't say what kind of accident, and the one time I asked her about it, she'd changed the subject, so I didn't ask again. I wish I had; it would have saved us a lot of heartache later on.

Raleigh lived a couple of miles outside of town, on the other side of the river. There wasn't even a road to his house, just a small, rickety bridge across the river, then a path through the woods. It sounded like that song ("Over the River and Through the Woods"), or the start of a fairy tale, like the troll who lived under the bridge in "The Three Billy Goats Gruff" ("Who's that trip-trapping over my bridge?"). Except then the path disappeared into a swamp (which I was sure must be full of bloodsuckers). Years ago, Mr. Wright had lost a cow, a Texas longhorn that he'd gotten somewhere (probably stolen), in that swamp, and it was never seen again. If I'd had to choose between Mr. Wright and that swamp, I would have taken the swamp, too, any day, though I would have loved to have seen a real Texas longhorn like the ones I saw in cowboy movies.

I'd never been to Raleigh's house and neither had any of the kids at school (who wants to slog through mud and bloodsuckers?), but that didn't stop them from making up all sorts of stories about it. The boys dared each other to go there, but none of them had done it. In my mind, I imagined it a ramshackle sort of place, but the kids at school had other ideas. Cora Young said Raleigh lived in a haunted house and that her cousin had gone there one Halloween night and was never seen again (that would have made a better story if we didn't all see her cousin bagging groceries every day at the store). Janine Perron thought Raleigh lived in a cardboard box, Dwight Randall thought he lived in an old railroad car (Dwight loved trains and was forever saying *he* was going to live in a caboose when he grew up), and Ronald Conley and Henry Souliere even got into a fight about it, Ronald being sure that Raleigh lived in an abandoned car, while Henry was just as sure that he lived in a tree house. Miss Paisley had made them both stay in at recess, and told them if they spent as much time studying as they did arguing, they just might pass a test once in a while. I thought that was only wishful thinking on Miss Paisley's part.

Whatever kind of house he lived in, Raleigh did catch fish out of the river and raise a few vegetables, but folks looked out for him, too, sending casseroles and baked goods home with him and giving him runt pigs to raise, or orphaned lambs. Just last week, Mrs. Wells had given him one of her chickens that had stopped laying.

"You can turn her into soup," she'd told Raleigh.

Folks in town found odd jobs for Raleigh. He rode with Mr. Hazelton early every morning, picking up the milk cans and taking them to the creamery. Mr. Gilpin let Raleigh work at the *Monitor* as a "printer's devil," which meant help-ing to print up the paper, setting type, sweeping up, and doing any odd job that needed doing. I wished I could be a printer's devil, too. It sounded like a lot more fun than farming.

But I didn't envy what Raleigh had to endure from the Wright brothers. They picked on him something awful, throwing stones and snowballs at him, knocking him down in the mud, and calling him the worst names. Raleigh could have whipped those brothers with one hand tied behind him, but he never fought back. Hannah called Raleigh "a gentle soul." Dennis and Wesley called him "yellow." The only thing that saved Raleigh was that he could run faster than both of them.

"Run, ya big chicken," they'd holler after him. "You're nothin' but a big yellow chicken."

Yellow or not, when it came to the Wright brothers, all I saw was *red*. They were meaner than hornets.

I'm sure Miss Paisley hadn't meant to, but she'd given them even more ammunition to use against Raleigh when she taught us fire safety. Dennis and Wesley were way more interested in *starting* fires than in *preventing* them, but at least Miss Paisley had their attention, especially when she told us how asbestos and gypsum board are two examples of fire retardants.

That sent Dennis and Wesley into peals of laughter.

"Retardants!" they'd hooted. "Must be talking about

Raleigh's family. I bet he has retard-aunts and retard-uncles both!"

Miss Paisley had kept the two of them after school, but that hadn't made a bit of difference, and I knew it was going to be a bad summer for Raleigh with Dennis and Wesley pestering him even worse than usual. With other kids who caused trouble, all that had to be done was to say something to their parents, but it didn't do any good to complain to Mr. Wright—he was meaner than Dennis and Wesley put together.

I should have run out and yelled at those Wright brothers, but I was afraid of what they'd do to *me*, so I hid in the bushes.

"Well, if it ain't the retardant," Dennis said.

The river was so shallow, Raleigh could have run across it. But he just stood there with the heron in his arms.

Dennis and Wesley advanced on Raleigh, and my knees felt wobbly. I wished this was a movie and Gary Cooper or Audie Murphy would ride in and rescue Raleigh. In the movies, you could always tell the good guys from the bad guys, and you knew the good guys would win. That wasn't true in real life.

"Put it down so we can finish it off," Dennis said. "That'll teach it not to steal our fish."

If anyone knew about stealing, it was Dennis and Wesley. They were practically experts.

Raleigh shook his head.

"Let it go, Retardant, or you'll be sorry," Dennis said.

"Yeah," said Wesley, "you'll be sorry."

Raleigh took a step toward the Wright brothers.

"Watch out," Wesley warned.

"Ah, he ain't gonna do anything," Dennis said. "He's too yellow."

"Yeah," said Wesley. "A yellow-bellied retard."

I clenched my fists and wished I could trounce them both. Our Sunday school teacher, Mrs. Hazelton, was always telling us that we were supposed to love thy neighbor, and to turn the other cheek. Well, I *didn't* love the Wright brothers, and I wished I could beat them up and see how *they* liked it. Even though they were bigger than me, and going into seventh grade, I think I could have beaten them up one at a time, in a fair fight, but if there was one thing you could count on with the Wright brothers, it was that they wouldn't play fair. While I was beating up one of them, the other would be hitting me over the head with a club.

Dennis shoved his nose in Raleigh's face.

"My dad says you ought to be locked up in a home for retards," Dennis said.

Last week's Sunday school story flashed through my head: David and Goliath.

I reached down, scooped up a stone, and flung it at Dennis. At least I *thought* I'd aimed it at Dennis.

The stone hit Raleigh right in the middle of his forehead.

"Hey! What's going on here?" Mr. Gilpin yelled behind me.

The Wright brothers skedaddled like wolves were after them.

Mr. Gilpin charged past me and steered Raleigh over to a rock. "Sit there for a minute and let your head clear," he said.

Mr. Gilpin looked at me and shook his head. "What were they thinking, throwing *stones*?" he said. "My word, they could have killed him!"

Mr. Gilpin thought the *Wright brothers* had hit Raleigh with the stone!

"Those ruffians," Mr. Gilpin went on. "They take after that reprobate of a father."

I didn't know what *reprobate* meant, but if Mr. Gilpin was using it to describe Mr. Wright, it couldn't be anything good. Hannah says if you don't have anything nice to say about a person, then don't say anything at all—so I won't say anything about Mr. Wright, except that he looked like the pigs he raised. Short, bristly hair circled his bald pink scalp, and he had a round, flat nose and beady red eyes. Whenever I saw him, I couldn't help thinking that it was better to have *no* father than a father like that. Hannah said Mr. Wright had "problems with the bottle," which Nadine said meant he was a drunk.

Mr. Gilpin pulled a handkerchief out of his pocket. He dipped it in the river and wiped the blood off Raleigh's forehead. Already, a lump was forming.

A lot of good that Sunday school story had done me, I thought.

"You're going to have a good-sized egg there," Mr. Gilpin said. "They come after you again, I'll brain them with my wooden leg."

Hannah had a painting of one of her Scottish ancestors charging English redcoats with an upraised broadsword (Hannah said it was called a claymore), and I could just picture Mr. Gilpin hopping after the Wright brothers brandishing his leg over his head.

That wooden leg fascinated me. I'd see it on Sunday afternoons when Mr. Gilpin came to the lake to swim. He'd show up in his old-fashioned bathing suit, unstrap his leg and lean it against a cedar tree, then hop to the water's edge, dive in, and swim all the way across the lake. Every Sunday I wanted to touch that wooden leg, but I didn't dare to. I was itching to know how Mr. Gilpin had lost his leg, but I didn't dare ask that, either.

"That was brave of you, Blue, stepping in to help Raleigh," Mr. Gilpin said. "You're a true-blue friend."

My face burned. What would Mr. Gilpin think if he knew *I* was the one who'd hit Raleigh?

"Blue True," Raleigh said, snuffling a little as he said

it. Raleigh didn't speak much, and when he did, he mixed up words.

"All right, a blue-true friend, then," Mr. Gilpin said, smiling at me while I felt my face getting hotter. Some friend I was! I was glad Raleigh couldn't tell on me.

I thought for sure that heron would be tearing chunks out of Raleigh's hands, but Raleigh whispered to it, and it stopped struggling.

"You could bring it to Hannah," I said. I was pretty sure Hannah had never taken care of a heron, but she'd nursed lots of animals back to health.

But Mr. Gilpin shook his head.

"It's got a broken wing," he said. "Won't be able to fly again. Best to put it out of its misery." He reached for the heron but jumped back as the heron's huge bill jabbed at him.

"Yikes!" Mr. Gilpin yelped. "I've already lost a leg. Don't care to lose a hand, too."

Raleigh whispered something to the heron, and it settled back into his arms.

"He might not be able to talk, but he's sure got a way with wild creatures," Mr. Gilpin said to me. "I can take care of that heron later. Those chicks, too. She won't be able to raise them, hurt like that, but right now, I think we need one of Hannah's doughnuts. How's that sound to you, Raleigh?"

Raleigh acted like he didn't even hear Mr. Gilpin and

just kept talking to the heron. Mr. Gilpin looked at me and shrugged. I picked up the bag of doughnuts I'd dropped and followed him into the *Monitor* office.

Mr. Gilpin's desk was covered with papers. It was always covered with papers—scribbled notes, stories he was working on, letters, ads, that sort of thing—but it seemed even more cluttered than usual.

"Celebration planning," Mr. Gilpin said.

Besides being owner and editor of the *Monitor*, Mr. Gilpin was also president of the historical society and head of the planning committee for the celebration. He'd been planning this celebration for months, writing skits (he called them pageants) that would show the important people and events in the town's history. I already knew some of the pageants he'd written because he'd been casting parts and handing out scripts for people to memorize. In one skit, Hannah was playing Woman No. 1.

"Hmph," Hannah had muttered. "Guess it'd be too much bother for him to give me a real name."

I didn't say so, but I felt the same way about Hannah naming me Blue. That was a *color*, not a real name.

Mr. Gilpin sat at his desk. He pushed the papers to one side and opened the bag of doughnuts. Most of them had gotten smashed when I dropped them, but Mr. Gilpin said his work crew would eat them anyway.

"Wouldn't want to waste Hannah's good doughnuts," he said.

Mr. Gilpin lit right into one, but I was still too upset to eat anything. It wasn't just because I'd hit Raleigh with the stone. It was Dennis saying Mr. Wright thought Raleigh should be locked up. Could Mr. Wright do that? Could he have Raleigh put away? I wanted to ask Mr. Gilpin that, too, but I always felt so tongue-tied around him.

Mr. Gilpin brushed the crumbs from his desk.

"Guess I'm going to have to have a talk with those boys," he said. "You never know. People *can* change."

The only way I could see the Wright brothers changing was if they got even *meaner*, but I didn't say that. And I didn't want Dennis and Wesley telling Mr. Gilpin that I was the one who'd hit Raleigh with the stone. He might not believe them, but still.

"Why didn't Raleigh just run across the river to get away from them?" I asked.

"Well, now, he couldn't have done that," Mr. Gilpin said. "You see, Raleigh almost drowned when he was a boy. Ever since then, he's been terrified of water."

I wanted to know how Raleigh had almost drowned (Hannah says I can ask questions till the cows come home), but Mr. Gilpin spoke first.

"Good thing you happened by when you did," Mr. Gilpin said. "Your arrival was fortuitous."

I didn't know what *fortuitous* meant, but if it had something to do with the Wright brothers, I wanted to get Mr. Gilpin's mind off having a talk with them.

21

"How much would it cost to put in an ad about a lost cat?" I asked. I had meant to ask him that. Really, I had.

"I don't charge for that," Mr. Gilpin said. He wrote "LOST, CAT" on the notepad on his desk.

"No," I said, "I mean we're wondering if someone *lost* a cat. There's one at the farm."

"Oh," Mr. Gilpin said, scribbling out "LOST" and writing "FOUND." "You should be more precise in your use of language, Blue."

I sighed. Mr. Gilpin sounded just like our teacher, Miss Paisley.

"Guess I'd better go take care of that heron, poor thing," Mr. Gilpin said, and I followed him outside, but there was no sign of Raleigh or the heron. The three baby herons in the nest were gone, too.

"Guess Raleigh took care of them himself," Mr. Gilpin said. "I'm sure it was hard for him, dispatching them. He's a sensitive person."

I wasn't sure what *dispatching* meant, but I figured it meant that heron and its babies were goners. I couldn't picture Raleigh dispatching them, either, but he'd taken Mrs. Wells's hen home to eat, and he'd raised runt pigs for bacon and ham, so he must know how.

I wished someone could dispatch the Wright brothers.

With all the excitement, Mr. Gilpin forgot to give me a nickel, so I had to ride home without any penny candy. It was past milking time, and I knew Hannah was waiting for me, but even so, I hesitated when I came to the fork in the road. To the left, I could see our farm, the lights twinkling in the barn where Hannah had probably already started milking. To the right was the lake.

I turned Dolly toward the lake and headed down the driveway to the Tilton camp. I'd seen a light in their window and knew they'd just arrived for the summer. If I hurried, I could get in a swim with Nadine before chores.

chapter 4

If the Wright brothers made me see red, with Nadine I was green with envy.

"Thou shalt not covet" was one of the commandments we'd learned in church, but it didn't mean anything to me until Hannah told me *covet* meant "to envy." Yes, I was guilty of that, at least sometimes, but I didn't want Nadine's *whole* life, just parts of it.

I couldn't remember a time when I *hadn't* known Nadine, and even though I only saw her in the summer, she was my best friend. Partly, that was because there weren't any other girls my age in school, and partly, it was because Nadine and I grew up together. Nadine was a year and a half older than me, but the Tiltons had been coming up ever since Nadine and I were babies, so we'd played together all our lives. Every summer, we just picked up where we'd left off, and every summer, Nadine reminded me that there was a whole other world out there beyond northern Vermont. She'd lived in Boston and New York, and now she lived near Washington, D.C. Nadine knew all about skyscrapers and subways and streetlights, things I'd only heard of. She'd visited the White House and the Capitol and the Washington and Lincoln monuments, and she had been to the Smithsonian about a zillion times, where she'd seen Orville and Wilbur Wright's plane, Charles Lindbergh's *Spirit of St. Louis,* and a plane like the one Amelia Earhart had been flying when she vanished. (I loved Amelia Earhart. She'd disappeared almost four and a half years before I was born, but even so, sometimes I dreamed that Amelia was my real mama and had left me before she headed off on her round-the-world flight.) Someday I wanted to fly round the world. Nadine had flown lots of places, like Paris and Rome. She'd even been to Hawaii!

Hannah said Nadine was spoiled. I wished I could be spoiled, too.

The farthest I'd ever been from home was when Hannah and I took the train up to Newport to Lake Memphremagog and I fell asleep *thinking* I'd seen the ocean.

Nadine went to a fancy school with hundreds of kids.

I went to Mud Island School, a one-room schoolhouse. There were only nineteen kids in the whole school, first through eighth grades. When classes started up in September, I'd be the only girl in fifth grade.

Nadine had after-school classes in ballet, piano, and something called elocution.

My after-school classes were milking, collecting eggs, filling the woodbox behind the stove, and shoveling snow.

I'd shown the school to Nadine one day as we were riding Dolly past and doing circus tricks (well, *I* was doing circus tricks—standing up on Dolly's back and then somersaulting off—but Nadine said I was just being dangerous). Nadine much preferred to pretend we were in the movie *National Velvet* (with Nadine as Elizabeth Taylor, of course). Nadine even looked a little like Elizabeth Taylor, but Dolly didn't look anything like her racehorse, Velvet.

Nadine couldn't get over how small the school was.

"It only has one room!" she exclaimed.

"I told you it's a *one-room* schoolhouse," I said.

"I know, but I didn't think you meant it," Nadine said. "Where do you go when you get sent to the principal's office?"

"We don't have a principal," I told her. "It's just Miss Paisley."

"Where do you go to the bathroom?" she wanted to know, so I led her to the outhouse behind the school.

Nadine's mouth dropped open.

"You have to go in there?" she whispered. "How positively provincial!"

Nadine was always throwing out big words I didn't know. She was twelve going on twenty, as Hannah liked to say. She was book-smart, but Nadine didn't know the first thing about making maple syrup (she couldn't even tell the difference between a red maple and a sugar maple), or how to milk a cow (she was too afraid of them to even *try*), or the difference between a Duchess apple and a Yellow Transparent. Nadine actually thought haying was *fun*, but that was only because she could go home when she was tired and didn't have to stick with it till it was all done.

Our rooms were as different as could be, too. Walking into Nadine's room was like being swept up into a swirl of cotton candy. Everything was pink—from the walls to her frilly bed to her closet filled with even frillier clothes—and her shelves were lined with dolls and Nancy Drew books. My room was like the outdoors: blue walls, a green braided rug, and shelves filled with birds' nests and rocks and my baseball card collection. I had a closet, but most of the time, my clothes were scattered around on the floor.

But as different as Nadine and I were, we had things in common too. We both liked movies and animals and being outdoors. S'mores and ice cream and ghost stories. Shooting stars and fireflies.

And Shadow Lake. Hardly a day went by that we didn't spend part of it either on or in the water: paddling the old canoe along the shoreline, fishing (though I had to put the worm on her hook and take off any fish she caught), or swimming (even though Nadine proclaimed the water to be "like ice" every time). We'd cannonball off the raft and play leapfrog and Marco Polo in the water until our skin was shriveled and our lips were blue. Nadine was a better swimmer than I was, because she'd had swimming lessons, in a pool, but I could hold my breath underwater a lot longer than she could, one reason being that Nadine hardly ever put her head underwater.

"You never know what's under there," she said, meaning fish, frogs, and crayfish. Nadine yelped every time anything so much as a minnow swam past her legs.

Nadine was right about the water being cold, too. She'd inch into the water, a step at a time, squealing like a pig, but I just dove in. Better to get it over quick.

That's how Nadine's older brother, Keith, swam, too. He'd barrel into the water, splashing us, which only made Nadine squeal louder.

"I'm telling Mom," Nadine shouted.

"Oh, for crying out loud, it's just water," Keith said. "C'mon, Blue, I'll race you to the raft."

I liked feeling I was part of Nadine's family, even if it was just for the summer. I especially loved the nights when I got to sleep over. Mr. Tilton would build us a campfire by the lake, and Nadine and I roasted marshmallows for s'mores and watched for shooting stars zipping across the sky. We lay tucked into musty army sleeping bags, slathered with bug repellent, whispering and giggling and telling ghost stories to each other until we were both too scared to sleep. One night, while Nadine was telling the story about the escaped murderer with a hook for an arm, Keith snuck up on us, and just as Nadine got to the part where the woman hears the *scrape, scrape, scrape* of the hook on the roof of the car, Keith tapped both of us on the shoulders. Nadine screamed so loud I thought they'd hear her in Canada, and I almost peed my pants. It was a long time before we forgave Keith, and an even longer time before we dared tell ghost stories again. Nadine was forever saying how she *wished* she were an only child, but I often wondered what it would be like to have a brother like Keith. He was tall and handsome, and told even scarier ghost stories than Nadine.

So I rode down the Tilton driveway, my stomach tumbling with excitement, and looking forward to a summer of swimming, picnics, camping out, baseball, and tons of talking and laughing with my best friend.

If I'd known how the summer was really going to turn out, I would have wheeled Dolly around and galloped in the other direction.

chapter 5

Mrs. Tilton and Nadine were just finishing supper when I arrived. Right away, I knew things were different.

For one, I hardly recognized Nadine; not only had she shot up about a foot, but she'd done something funny with her hair. She'd always had a ponytail; now she looked like she had a Pekingese perched on her head. Second, Nadine didn't squeal and hug me the way she always did. Third, she and Mrs. Tilton were the only ones at the table.

Mr. Tilton wouldn't be here for the summer, Mrs. Tilton said, what with the war and work he had to do for the government. Keith wouldn't be coming up, either. He'd joined the army and was over fighting in Korea.

I could hardly imagine a summer without both of them, but I tried not to show how disappointed I was. It wouldn't be the same without Keith telling ghost stories, or scaring us, or racing me to the raft, but at least Nadine and I would have a good time together.

"Sit down and join us," Mrs. Tilton said. "You must be starved."

"Yes, ma'am," I said. "Feels like my belly button's trying to shake hands with my backbone."

Mrs. Tilton laughed and shook her head.

"You Vermonters have such quaint expressions," she said. I didn't know what *quaint* meant, but I just smiled and sat down while Mrs. Tilton fixed a plate for me.

"I hope you like chicken divan," she said.

I hoped I did, too. Mrs. Tilton served a lot of food I'd never even heard of, things like artichokes and Roquefort cheese and eggplant Parmesan. Nadine swore they even ate snails, but thank goodness Mrs. Tilton had never put any of those in front of me.

Mrs. Tilton wasn't like anybody I'd ever seen in real life. She was more like a movie star, tall and willowy and glamorous, like Lana Turner, and she talked with a French accent. She painted her fingernails and wore makeup, even during the week! She wore clothes that no one around here wore, like scarves (not wool ones, either) and pants that weren't overalls but were made out of some whispery fabric that shimmered when she moved.

"Not very practical," Hannah'd say, and I'd nod. They weren't practical at all, and that's what I loved about them.

All my clothes were either handmade or hand-me-downs, stained and mended, and I always bit my lip when I saw Nadine and Mrs. Tilton wearing matching mother-daughter outfits.

Nadine seemed to fit right in at our house, but I always felt embarrassed to have Mrs. Tilton over, seeing our shabby furniture, the worn linoleum on the kitchen floor, and the peeling wallpaper, and I felt uncomfortable having her eat with us. Hannah was a good cook, but she made things like tuna pea wiggle, dried beef gravy, and shepherd's pie (I just couldn't see Mrs. Tilton eating tuna pea wiggle, on crackers, off a chipped plate), and Hannah didn't get all worked up if there happened to be a hair in the mashed potatoes ("Just pick it out, it won't kill you," Hannah'd say). Seeing Mrs. Tilton and Hannah side by side was like sitting a sleek, shiny barn swallow next to a hen. Nadine complained about her family, but I didn't see what she had to complain about. To have a mother like that, and a dad, *and* a brother . . . some people are just plain lucky.

I dug into the chicken divan. Mrs. Tilton wasn't the cook Hannah was (though you knew you'd never find a hair in your food, either), but it tasted good just the same. I drank three glasses of water too (at home, Hannah and I always drank milk, but I felt funny asking Mrs. Tilton for milk instead of water).

"My goodness, you're thirsty," Mrs. Tilton said, filling my glass again.

I nodded.

"I feel completely rizzared," I said.

She stopped pouring.

"Rizzared?" she said.

"It means 'all dried up'—you know, like a raisin," I said.

Mrs. Tilton smiled.

"I'll have to tell Keith that, in my next letter," she said.

Her mentioning Keith reminded me how strange it seemed not to have Mr. Tilton and Keith eating with us. That's one of the things I'd always loved about being at Nadine's, all of us eating together, Mr. and Mrs. Tilton talking about politics, or an art exhibit they wanted to see, or places I'd never heard of, like Naples and Machu Picchu, and Keith would be cracking us up with knock-knock jokes. At home, meals were awfully quiet with just me and Hannah. Mrs. Tilton seemed quieter than usual, too, but it was probably because she was worried about Keith.

Mrs. Tilton wasn't the only one being quiet. I kept glancing at Nadine, wondering why she wasn't talking a mile a minute, like usual.

"A lot of deliveries today?" Mrs. Tilton asked.

I nodded, and swallowed quick so's I wouldn't have to talk with my mouth full.

"Mrs. Wells, the *Monitor*, and the Trombleys," I said. I didn't mention anything about Raleigh or the Wright brothers.

"How's he doing, the poor man?" Mrs. Tilton asked,

meaning Mr. Trombley. "Hannah told me about his accident in her Christmas card."

"He's still dwably," I said. That was a word Hannah used when someone was sickly.

Mrs. Tilton laughed.

"*Rizzared* and now *dwably*," Mrs. Tilton said. "Sometimes I feel like I need a Scottish dictionary to figure out what you're talking about up here!"

I didn't tell Mrs. Tilton that we sometimes had trouble understanding her accent, too.

"They must be having a hard time, him being laid up this long," she said.

"I just left off a whole hamper of food there," I said.

"That Hannah," Mrs. Tilton said, shaking her head. "She's always helping out others."

"Yes, ma'am," I said. I didn't tell her I was mad at Hannah and Mr. Trombley both. Hannah and I'd been saving for months, trying to tuck away enough money to take a trip to Prince Edward Island, but after Mr. Trombley got hurt, Hannah knew they couldn't pay the hospital bills, so she'd put all the money we'd saved into an envelope and left it in their mailbox. That way, they wouldn't know who'd done it.

"I'm sorry, Blue," Hannah had said, "but I wouldn't be able to enjoy myself knowing how much they needed the money."

"That's what I love about this place, the *neighborliness*," Mrs. Tilton went on. "Everyone helping out everyone else."

Well, in my opinion, sometimes they helped each other out *too* much.

"I know I never would have survived those first summers here without Hannah," Mrs. Tilton said. "Nadine was such a colicky baby, and her crying was driving me to distraction. Hannah knew just how to calm her."

Nadine rolled her eyes.

"Please, Mother," she said. "Do you have to tell that story every summer?"

Since when had Nadine started calling Mrs. Tilton Mother? I wondered. Before, she'd always called her Mama. And she'd always loved it when Mrs. Tilton or Hannah told stories about her. One thing you could say for Nadine, she liked being the center of attention.

I liked those stories, too, of how Hannah plunked us down together on a quilt while she picked berries, or set us in a laundry basket while she milked cows. Mrs. Tilton marveled at how Hannah could tend babies and do farm chores all at the same time.

I set down my fork and looked at Nadine.

"How about a swim before chores?" I asked.

"I don't think so," Nadine said. "The water would absolutely ruin my hairdo."

My mouth fell partway open. Nothing had ever kept us

from swimming her first night here. When had Nadine started worrying about her hair?

"You could borrow my bathing cap," Mrs. Tilton told her.

A bathing cap? The only people I knew who wore bathing caps were Hannah and the old ladies in her quilting group.

Nadine rolled her eyes again and shook her head, making her hairdo look like a wet dog shaking itself.

"Too bad there isn't a pool here," she said. "Back home, my friends and I hang out at the pool all day long."

I stared at her as if she had two heads. Why would anyone want to swim in a pool instead of a big, beautiful lake?

I went home wondering what had happened to Nadine. I'd seen enough science-fiction movies over the years for me to entertain the idea that aliens had come and switched bodies with her, and to wonder if Martians were holding the real Nadine on a spaceship somewhere in our galaxy.

chapter 6

The next morning, while Hannah and I were weeding the garden, I was still worrying about whether Nadine was an alien or not, and how I could tell, when I saw her biking up our driveway. Her hair was back in a ponytail, so maybe this was the real Nadine.

I studied her as she hopped off the bike and opened the gate to the garden, looking for clues. The real Nadine had a small mole on her left ankle, but that didn't help me, because the Nadine coming into the garden had on ankle socks. I'd have to be clever and ask her something that only the real Nadine would know.

Nadine said she'd come to help us weed, which made me suspicious; in *The Thing from Another World*, the alien was a frozen vegetable, so I watched to make sure Nadine wasn't trying to give secret messages to the carrots and squash.

At first, Nadine seemed like her old self, and a wave of relief washed over me. Maybe all she'd needed was to be *here*, to be reminded of what she'd always loved about our summers together, but the more Nadine talked, the more I realized that instead of coming to help weed, she'd only come over to brag.

First, she talked about all her friends back home, which just made me mad. I didn't talk about my friends with *her*. Well, I didn't really have any other friends, but still. If I had, I wouldn't have mentioned them in front of her.

Then Nadine went on and on about the article she was writing for her school newspaper on England's new queen, Elizabeth II, and the coronation, which wouldn't be until next year, and wouldn't it be just divine to be able to go to the coronation, and what she'd wear if she could go, and then she went on about how she'd already received special mention for an article she'd written on Edward, Duke of Windsor, and Wallis Simpson, and wasn't it just so romantic and tragic how Edward had had to choose between the throne and the woman he loved, and he'd given up being king so that he could marry Wallis.

I snuck a glance at Hannah. When we'd heard of King George's death on the radio in February, Hannah had said it was a good thing George had been king during the war instead of Edward because Edward and Wallis were nothing more than a couple of shallow, self-centered ninnies.

The corner of Hannah's mouth turned up in the faintest

of smiles, but she just kept pulling weeds and didn't say a word.

I was pretty sure an alien wouldn't be interested in Edward and Wallis, so I gave up on that idea, but why was Nadine interested? The old Nadine wouldn't have given a hoot about that stuff. It wasn't like they were her family, and all that had happened before Nadine and I were even born, but I wasn't about to say that to the new Nadine. I just knew she would have gotten all huffy.

"You know, some of my ancestors were kings and queens," Nadine said, as if reading my mind. "I had an ancestor on the *Mayflower*, too."

Not knowing who my parents were meant I didn't know any of my ancestors, either. When my real mama came back, that was one of the things I wanted to ask her (along with some of the more important stuff, like why she left me in the first place).

"Did you know that, in England, they celebrate every king and queen's birthday in June, no matter when they were born?" Nadine said.

I looked at Hannah. Was that true? Nadine had always been a walking encyclopedia, but sometimes it was hard to tell if she was just making things up.

"They've done that since the 1700s," Nadine went on. "It's called Trooping the Color, except in England, they spell *color* with a *u: c-o-l-o*-u-*r.*"

She was a walking dictionary, too. I couldn't help but

think how much easier spelling tests would be if I could just add letters to a word whenever I felt like it.

"My birthday's already in June," Nadine said, "so if I ever become queen, I won't have to change it. Isn't that handy?"

Hannah made a funny sound in her throat, and the corner of her mouth twisted a little higher.

I knew some girls dreamed of being a princess (I wasn't one of them), but leave it to the new Nadine to want to be the queen.

Nadine rattled off all the things she'd put on her birthday wish list, things that the old Nadine would have made fun of, like high heels, gloves, and makeup. I would never have put any of those on a wish list, but then, I never made lists for birthdays or Christmas. Why ask for things you know you're not going to get?

I'd always wished my birthday were in the summer instead of December, where it seemed to get forgotten because of Christmas. Nadine's birthday was June 30, and her family always made a big deal out of it, taking her out to eat at a restaurant *and* having a party at home, with party hats and streamers, a piñata filled with candy, a five-layer cake and three kinds of ice cream, and tons of presents. I'd never even eaten in a restaurant before. Hannah had always celebrated my birthday on December 5 (with a small cake and homemade ice cream, which was better than store-bought, but still), but that was only because Dr. Hastings had said he *thought* I was two days old when Hannah found me on December 7, so it was only a guess.

As soon as Nadine finished telling us her birthday list, she went home, complaining about how hot it was. I watched her go, thinking she hadn't done enough work to *get* hot, and mad that she could just leave when she wanted to, when she hollered over her shoulder.

"Come by later for a swim," she said, which made my heart soar. The new Nadine was going to take some getting used to, but she was still my best friend.

She was right, too. It was plenty hot—*muithy*, Hannah called it. (Hannah had about a thousand words to describe weather. I took it the Scottish people talked about weather a lot, just like Vermonters.)

I wished I could just leave, too, but we still had the carrots, beets, and potatoes to do. I couldn't help thinking how much cooler it would have been on Prince Edward Island, with a breeze blowing in off the ocean. If it weren't for the Trombleys, we would have been there right now.

"Stop being glumshous," Hannah said, reading my mind. "They would have done the same for us, you know."

Glumshous means "sulky," and it was something Hannah couldn't abide. I wasn't allowed to whine, pout, *or* sulk. There was a long list of things Hannah couldn't abide, like lying, rudeness, and laziness. And weeds.

41

I wiped the sweat from my forehead and looked down the road. I wouldn't have to work so hard when my real mama came.

I wondered if not telling Hannah my secret about watching for my mama could be considered lying. I hadn't actually *told* a lie, but maybe *not* telling was a kind of lie, too.

We finished up in the garden and I'd hoped I could fit in a swim with Nadine before chores (unless she'd done up her hair again), but Hannah said we'd have just enough time to milk before her weekly quilting club meeting. All through milking, I thought longingly about diving off Nadine's dock into that cold water. I'd go over there after Hannah left for her meeting. I was sure if I could get Nadine swimming, and laughing, I could coax out the old Nadine.

On the way to the house, I checked the bowl I'd left for the cat and saw it'd been licked clean. She'd found the milk after all.

At supper, I was as hungry as a pack of jackals, but I left some chicken and biscuit on my plate.

"Boy, am I full," I said, patting my stomach. "Can't eat another bite."

Hannah kept right on eating.

"I don't suppose that eat has anything to do with you leaving food on your plate all of a sudden?" she said.

I sighed. Fooling Hannah was harder than teaching a frog to play a fiddle.

"Yes, ma'am," I said, and Hannah smiled.

"You can give her some of my chicken, too," she said. She had a soft heart, that Hannah. It was that soft heart that had made her give our trip money to the Trombleys. But I also knew that soft heart had made her take *me* in, too.

Hannah went off to her weekly quilting club meeting while I washed the dishes. I turned on the radio to hear *Fibber McGee and Molly*, but instead President Truman was talking about sending more troops into Korea, so I turned it off and took the bowl of chicken out to leave for the cat.

The night air was so chilly I changed my mind about swimming. Nadine wouldn't go in, with it being this cold, and I didn't feel much like it anymore, either. I stood looking up into the starry night and listened to the bullfrogs sing from the lake.

Overhead, the Milky Way looked like a river flowing through the dark sky, and the stars hung so low and bright it seemed I could catch them on my tongue, like snowflakes. I wrapped one of Hannah's quilts around me and sat on the porch in the starlight, hoping to get a glimpse of the cat. I fell asleep without seeing her, but the bowl was empty in the morning.

chapter 7

Sundays were a day of rest, so in the summer, after chores and milking, and two long (and I mean *loooong*) hours of church and Sunday school, I'd always spent the whole afternoon with Nadine. Mostly we swam, but sometimes we wrote and put on plays, or took picnics up Black Hill, or rode Dolly and played cowboys and Indians. Sometimes we stopped by the town ball field and watched the old-timers play.

"I can't believe you're not allowed to play baseball or cards on Sunday," Nadine said. "I'm glad I'm not a Presbyterian."

I hated having to dress up for church (I was sure God wouldn't mind if I wore my overalls, but Hannah didn't see it that way), and it was awfully dull sitting through Reverend Miller's sermons, but when Nadine described her church—first Communion, confession, and how she had to give up her favorite things, like candy and ice cream, for Lent—well, I thought I was getting off easy being a Presbyterian. And the best thing about church was that the Wright brothers weren't there. I figured even God would keel over if the Wright brothers ever showed up.

The old Nadine had liked baseball, even though she wasn't very good at it, but the new Nadine acted as if it bored her, so I didn't linger long at the ball field, even though I wanted to. I loved baseball. I was the best player at school, and always got picked captain when we were choosing teams, and Hannah and I listened to Red Sox games on the radio. Sometimes Nadine would toss a ball with me, but I mostly ended up chasing after it. Nadine threw, well, like a girl.

We could always count on Raleigh being at the ball field too, seeing as how both teams let him be their batboy, and like always, he came running over to me.

"Blue True," he said.

"Why's he call you that?" Nadine asked.

"I think he's trying to say *true-blue*," I answered. I hadn't told her about the Wright brothers and the heron. "He's just got it backward."

Raleigh stood patting Dolly until Esther Green came by pushing her baby, Rodney, in his stroller to watch her husband play ball. Rodney was just about the homeliest thing I'd ever seen, but Esther seemed to like him.

Raleigh liked him, too. He liked all babies. He'd rush

45

over to pick up Rodney, cuddling and cooing and making faces to get Rodney to smile. The way Raleigh held Rodney reminded me of how he'd cradled that hurt heron.

Nadine wrinkled her nose.

"That Raleigh gives me the creeps," she said. "I wouldn't let him anywhere near *my* baby."

I stared at her, too shocked to say anything. The old Nadine would never have said something so mean. Raleigh couldn't help being the way he was.

When Rodney started to cry, Raleigh put him over his shoulder and jostled Rodney up and down, patting him gently on the bottom until he stopped crying.

I felt my eyes sting. Even Raleigh knew how to take care of a baby. Why hadn't my own mama been able to do it?

"What's the matter?" Nadine asked.

"Nothing," I answered, blinking fast. "Let's go."

Besides me not being allowed to play baseball on Sundays, Nadine couldn't believe that I didn't get an allowance. I hadn't even known what an allowance was until I'd met Nadine. Nadine didn't have any chores, and she still got an allowance, and if Mrs. Tilton asked her to do a chore, Nadine could usually get out of it by faking being sick. Mrs. Tilton would ask her to pick up her socks, and Nadine would groan and say her stomach hurt "something terrible." Mrs. Tilton would feel Nadine's head, cluck "Poor baby" a few times, and make her some chamomile tea.

Hannah would never have fallen for that. I'd tried once, on a day when we were to have a vocabulary test, moaning and saying I felt sick. Hannah hadn't said a word, just set the bottle of castor oil up on the cookstove to warm, and I'd scuttled off to school. I didn't dread vocabulary tests nearly as much as I dreaded castor oil.

Nadine had her mother wrapped around her little finger, but she and her mom had fun, too, little things like making cookies and cupcakes, and big things like taking trips to Montreal to eat out, visit the botanical gardens, and shop for new dresses. I didn't like cooking, and hated dresses with a passion, but I envied the time they spent together. Mrs. Tilton had invited me along once, last summer, but Hannah and I'd had hay to get in. I was hoping they'd invite me again this summer. I'd never been to Montreal. Nadine said everyone spoke French up there. If I went with them, I'd try out a little of the Quebecois French I'd learned from listening to the kids at school.

Nadine's father could be really fun, too. Besides teaching us how to build a campfire, he'd taken us fishing (Nadine hated worms and cleaning fish, but I didn't mind), showed us how to do jackknives and back dives off the raft, and even taught us Morse code. He taught us how to dance, too. Nadine and I were more interested in the jitterbug and swing than in slow dances (who wanted to hold hands and dance close with a boy, anyway?), but when I watched Nadine stand on her daddy's feet while they waltzed around the kitchen, I felt tears prickling my eyes and had to bite my lip. What would it be like to dance with *my* daddy? I wondered.

Some nights, when we were lying out under the stars, Nadine and I played "What's your favorite thing?"

"Favorite food?" Nadine would ask.

It was always hard to pick just one.

"Sugar on snow," I decided. "Green apples, too."

Eating green apples always made Nadine's mouth pucker up, and she didn't like it that she wasn't here in the spring when we were sugaring, so she'd never tasted sugar on snow.

"Well, mine is peach cobbler and pecan pie," she said. She knew I'd never had those, either.

"Favorite smell?" I asked next.

"The ocean," Nadine said.

I'd never been to the ocean, so I didn't know it had a smell all its own.

"Mine is lilacs," I said. "And fresh-cut hay."

"My favorite *sound* is the ocean, too," Nadine said.

"Mine is spring peepers," I said. "And Canada geese. And cowbells."

Hannah heard us one night and said her favorite sound was her grandfather playing the bagpipes. I wished I could have heard that, so that could be *my* favorite sound, too.

Somehow, I didn't think the new Nadine would want to

play "What's your favorite thing?" this summer, and if she did, I had a feeling her answers would be very different.

When I fed the cat that night, I wondered how she would answer if she could.

"What's *your* favorite sound?" I asked her, then answered in a high voice.

"Mice squeaking," I said.

The cat tilted her head to one side, listening.

"And what's your favorite smell?" I asked her, answering again in the high voice.

"Mouse pie!" I said.

My bark of laughter scared her, and she dashed off.

"Well, if you didn't want to play, you could have just said so," I called after her.

I didn't see Nadine again until Friday. With three days of dry weather, Hannah and I worked straight through haying. I didn't even have time to go swimming, but Friday was raining, so I got to spend that whole day with Nadine. (Rain on the roof was one of my favorite sounds, too. I couldn't have told you whether it was really the sound or because it meant that we couldn't hay.)

She seemed like the old Nadine again (I'd come up with another idea to explain her two personalities—maybe Mr. Tilton was working on a secret government formula, and Nadine accidently drank some, and now she was two people in one, like Dr. Jekyll and Mr. Hyde), and I thought

I'd better enjoy the old Nadine while I could. We played Chinese checkers and Monopoly, Old Maid, and Go Fish, and played every one of her records on the hand-cranked Victrola. Then we were out of things to do.

"Let's go up in the attic," I suggested. I loved snooping through boxes and trunks to see what treasures other people had in their attics.

Even the old Nadine was scared of attics and cellars (she hated mice, and spiders, and bugs of any kind), but she didn't like to admit it, and since she couldn't think of anything better to do, she shrugged and followed me up the stairs.

chapter 8

It was dark and dusty up there, like most attics, with boxes that mice had chewed into, a chair with a broken armrest, picture frames, and piles of crumbling books. We found an old trunk. Nadine tried to scare me by saying there might be a body in it, just like in *Arsenic and Old Lace*, but all we found was worn-out dresses and hats. They were faded and smelled musty, but we tried them on anyway, laughing at each other, and it felt like old times. At first, we pretended to be the crazy elderly aunts in *Arsenic and Old Lace*, then Nadine threw a feather boa around her neck and strutted across the attic like Bette Davis.

The lace around my collar was scratchy, and I tugged at it.

"Boy, I'm glad we don't have to wear clothes like this anymore," I said. I liked my frayed shirts and faded overalls.

Nadine didn't say anything, but I could tell from the

way she twirled the skirts back and forth that she would have loved to wear clothes like that *all* the time.

We put the clothes back in the trunk and snooped in some of the boxes, but there wasn't anything interesting in them, just Christmas ornaments and some old dishes wrapped in crumpled-up newspapers (I didn't tell Nadine that the mice had made nests in them). We played with the spinning wheel, which made me think of a propeller on an airplane.

"Let's play we're paratroopers, dropped behind enemy lines," I suggested, and I thought Nadine was going to go for it, but when she saw that meant crawling on our bellies across the dirty attic floor, she changed her mind.

Instead, she picked up one of the magazines, an old *Reader's Digest.*

"We can play school," Nadine said. "I'll be the teacher and see how many of the words you know from 'It Pays to Increase Your Word Power.'"

I stared at her in disbelief. The old Nadine would never have suggested that; she knew how much I hated school, especially vocabulary tests.

I never did well on Miss Paisley's vocabulary tests. We had to give both the correct spelling *and* the definition, so I was pretty much doomed from the start. I was always getting mixed up on words like *receive, niece,* and *sleigh* and all those rules to follow like "*i* before *e* except after *c*," and those were easy compared to the ones Miss Paisley gave us, words like *propitious* and *pernicious* and *perspicacious*, which doesn't have anything to do with perspiration, but it should. That word made me sweat just *hearing* it! *Perspicacious* means "having keen judgment or understanding," but I couldn't figure out why we needed to know words like *perspicacious*. I'd never heard *anyone* use that word, and it seemed to me that if you *had* keen judgment, you wouldn't be throwing around a word like *perspicacious*, which probably gave you a good chance of getting a knuckle sandwich. I mean, I couldn't exactly see myself saying to Dennis or Wesley Wright, "It would not be perspicacious of you to steal my lunchbox."

Perspicacious had thrown me into such a panic that when I remembered how Sally Morley's nosebleed had made Robert Perkins faint dead away and Miss Paisley had been so busy tending to both of them that she'd given us recess the rest of the afternoon, I figured I had nothing to lose and closed my eyes, leaned sideways, and landed with a thud on the floor.

Sally gasped, and little Mary Richardson started crying, but Miss Paisley didn't even look up from her desk.

"We can do without your histrionics, Blue," she said.

Apparently, I had not been perspicacious enough to realize Miss Paisley wouldn't fall for that. At least she didn't put *histrionics* on the test, but I got a C— anyway.

Miss Paisley also threw words like *ptarmigan* at us. How's a body to know that *ptarmigan* has a silent *p* at the start? After that, when she said *tolerant*, I thought, Aha! She's trying to fool us. It must have a silent *p*, too.

It doesn't. I got a D+ on that test.

I thought Miss Paisley should be more tolerant about letting me spell words the way I wanted. If the English could throw in extra letters, why couldn't I?

So you can see why I was *not* interested in "It Pays to Increase Your Word Power."

"*Crepuscular*," Nadine said. "Does it mean (a) having to do with an infection, (b) pertaining to the abdomen, (c) happening at twilight, or (d) absorbent?"

It sounded like a word Miss Paisley would give us, but I couldn't remember ever hearing it, so I chose (a).

"Nope," said Nadine. "Twilight. Fireflies are crepuscular insects, for example."

The only person I could imagine *using* a word like *crepuscular* was Miss Paisley. Or Nadine. Or Mr. Gilpin.

"Okay, how about *auspicious*?" Nadine said.

I was pretty sure Miss Paisley *had* put *auspicious* on a vocabulary test, but I couldn't remember what it meant.

"Somebody who's guilty?" I said.

"Wrong," said Nadine. "You're thinking *suspicious*. *Auspicious* means 'promising' or 'encouraging,' like an auspicious beginning."

"Beginning of what?" I muttered, but Nadine ignored me.

I found out that *avuncular* meant "being like an uncle,"

cantankerous was another word for "crabby" or "cranky," and *filch* meant "to steal something of little value."

"Wow," said Nadine. "I can't believe you haven't gotten a single one right."

I was beginning to feel cantankerous with both *Reader's Digest* and Nadine and didn't want to play the game anymore, but Nadine was just getting started.

"For Christmas, I got a book on phobias," Nadine said. "Do you know anyone with a phobia, a fear of something?"

I was afraid of the Wright brothers and vocabulary tests, but those probably didn't count as real phobias. I'd never told Nadine about my fear of clowns, even though the old Nadine wouldn't have made fun of me.

I wasn't so sure about the new Nadine.

"Raleigh's afraid of water," I said. I didn't really feel right telling her that, but I didn't see how it would hurt.

"That's hydrophobia," Nadine crowed. "It's another name for rabies, because animals that have rabies are afraid of water. It makes them choke. Then there's lygophobia, that's fear of the dark, and ophidiophobia, fear of snakes"— Nadine shuddered when she said that—"and phalacrophobia is the fear of becoming bald. Triskaidekaphobia is the fear of the number thirteen, pupaphobia is the fear of puppets, and gephyrophobia is the fear of crossing bridges. I could tell you all of them."

She would have, too, if Mrs. Tilton hadn't called us

down for lunch. That was another thing different about Nadine's family. What they called lunch was our dinner, and their dinner was our supper.

As soon as Nadine turned to go downstairs, I filched one of the *Reader's Digest*s and crammed it into my waistband. My plan was to memorize all the words in "It Pays to Increase Your Word Power," and next time we played, I'd show Nadine she wasn't the only one who could throw around big words.

As I turned to follow Nadine, a word on one of the crumpled-up newspapers caught my eye: STOLEN! I tucked the piece of paper in my pocket and went down to lunch.

Mrs. Tilton had our plates all ready at our places. I slid into my chair and picked up my fork. Nadine used hers to prod the suspicious lump on her plate.

"Don't poke at your food, Nadine," Mrs. Tilton said. "It's not polite."

"What is it?" Nadine asked.

"Waldorf salad," Mrs. Tilton said. "I thought we'd have something nice and light."

I'd never heard of Waldorf salad, and even though it didn't look like any salad I'd ever seen, I liked salads, so I took a bite. I'd only chewed twice before I realized I was in trouble. Not only was I going to have a hard time *getting* the food down, I was going to have a hard time *keeping* it down.

Apples, celery, grapes, and walnuts, all together in one

dish. I loved fruit, and I loved vegetables; I just didn't like them mixed together, and to make it even worse, they were covered with mayonnaise.

Mrs. Tilton chattered on, not noticing my distress.

"I'm fixing sautéed sweetbreads for dinner," Mrs. Tilton said. "Have you had them before, Blue?"

I gave my head a little shake, afraid of spewing Waldorf salad all over her.

"Well, I hope you'll join us later and try them," Mrs. Tilton said. "I think it's important to try new things."

Mrs. Tilton went into the pantry to get a pitcher of ice water, and I spit the Waldorf salad into my napkin. I'd worry about how to dispose of it later.

Nadine looked at me, her eyebrows arched.

"I bet you don't know what sweetbreads are, do you?" she said.

No, I didn't even know what sweetbreads were, but if they were like Hannah's cinnamon bread or her currant scones, I was sure they would be good. I wished I were home right now, having some of those scones with Hannah.

"It's the organs of an animal," Nadine said, "heart, pancreas, and throat." And she watched with satisfaction as the taste of Waldorf salad came back up in my throat. Hannah ate chicken giblets and cow's tongue (being Scottish, she didn't like to waste anything), and it sometimes seemed to me that she would have eaten every scrap of animal if she could, right down to the hide. Maybe that's why she liked tripe, which was cow's stomach. She'd made me take a bite once, just to try it. It tasted like a wet leather shoe. I would rather have eaten the shoe. But as far as I knew, Hannah had never eaten sweetbreads.

The Waldorf salad lunch was bad enough. I knew I was going to dream up a good excuse as to why I couldn't come to supper.

That night, I carried a saucer of milk out to the cat. She was waiting by the barn. I took a step toward her, but she ducked behind the hay rake and wouldn't come out until I set the saucer down and backed away. I could tell she didn't like me being there, but hunger made her brave (or intrepid, as I'd learned from "It Pays to Increase Your Word Power"). She crept toward the bowl.

"Just be glad it's not sweetbreads," I told her, though when I thought about it, it made sense to feed sweetbreads to cats. Or dogs.

Just not humans.

I squatted down beside the cat, as close as she'd let me, and tried out my other new words on her while she ate. If she already knew that *contumacious* meant "rebellious," or that *anserous* was "being silly like a goose," she didn't let on.

When I stood up, a crinkly sound in my pocket reminded me of the piece of newspaper I'd stuffed there. I pulled it from my pocket and smoothed it out.

It was just the corner of one page, only part of the story, about a camel and monkey missing from the small traveling circus that had come through town.

I remembered that circus—I was five when Hannah had taken me (that's where I'd seen the woman doing acrobatic tricks on a horse)—and I remembered seeing a monkey and the trapeze artist, but I didn't remember hearing anything about any missing animals.

I slipped the piece of paper back into my pocket.

chapter 9

I didn't get to try my new words on Nadine the next day because the rain stopped and Hannah and I cut more hay. Hannah let me do the mowing. I was nervous at first, but Dolly knew what to do, and we went round and round the upper field until my backside was numb from being bounced on the hard iron seat of the mower. My hands were stiff from holding the reins all afternoon, too, but milking helped work the soreness out of them.

"Move over, Daisy," I said, slapping her on the rump. I'd named the cows after flowers in Hannah's garden. Besides Daisy, there was Rose, Iris, Peony, Tulip, Daffodil, and Chrysanthemum (the way her hair swirled in the middle of her forehead reminded me of a chrysanthemum). So far, Miss Paisley hadn't given us *chrysanthemum* on one of our spelling tests, but I was sure she would. I'd be in trouble, too, when she did, because I didn't have any idea how to spell it. But I thought it made a nice name.

For a cow.

Sitting there milking, my head resting against the cow, listening to the sound of the milk hitting the pail, I almost fell asleep, but then I felt a prickly sensation come over me, a feeling that I was being watched. I glanced over my shoulder and saw the cat in the open doorway. I stood up, and she turned and ran. I poured some milk into a bowl and set it by the doorway, just in case she came back later.

By the time I'd finished milking Chrysanthemum, the sun was setting, and Hannah and I were so tired we had just crackers and milk for supper. I knew Mrs. Tilton would never serve crackers and milk for supper, and Nadine said it was something only *prisoners* would eat, but I liked it. All you had to do was crush up saltine crackers in a bowl and pour milk on them. I carried my bowl out to the porch and sat on the steps to eat.

Across the yard, I could see the cat lapping milk (no crackers) out of the bowl I'd left for her. She picked her head up and stared at me. I could see drops of milk on her whiskers.

"You know, I was left, too," I told her.

Hannah came out and stood behind me.

"She's awfully skinny, poor thing," she said. "Looks like she had kittens recently, too."

I wondered how Hannah could tell that.

"I haven't seen any kittens," I said.

"She's probably hidden them," Hannah said.

I went and got the flashlight and searched every inch of the barn, but I didn't find any kittens. I searched the toolshed and garage, too.

"They may have died," Hannah said. "She's so small and thin she may not have had enough milk to feed them."

That made me feel sad.

"I wish she'd let me pet her," I said.

"Give her time," Hannah said. "She has to learn to trust you."

"How could someone just leave her?" I asked. It was the same question I wanted to ask the woman who'd left me in Hannah's kettle ten and a half years ago.

"Some folks don't think of anything but themselves," Hannah said. "There's lots of glundies in this world."

Glundie is another word for "fool." So are *gowk*, *coof*, *dobbie*, and *tattie*. *Tattie* also means "potatoes," and we had tatties and neeps many nights for supper. Neeps are turnips. I didn't care for turnips, and neither did Nadine, but she loved saying *tatties* and *neeps*. Nadine loved Hannah's Scottish words ("She's even better than 'It Pays to Increase Your Word Power,'" Nadine said), and she'd giggle every morning when, instead of calling us lazy-bones, Hannah would holler up the stairs, "Up, you two snoofmadrunes!" I liked the Scottish words, too. Maybe it was because I didn't have to spell them.

Thinking about those Scottish words gave me an idea. I'd been wondering what I'd give Nadine for her birthday (not having any money meant my presents always had to be homemade). Mrs. Tilton had said she needed a Scottish dictionary to understand me and Hannah; I'd make Nadine a dictionary of Scottish words!

chapter 10

It was just the four of us for Nadine's birthday. "An all-girls party," Mrs. Tilton said, and Nadine smiled, but it was her fake smile, and I knew she was upset that her dad wasn't there. I knew that Keith was over in Korea, but I'd thought Mr. Tilton would at least show up. He'd never missed her birthday before.

Because Mr. Tilton and Keith weren't there, Nadine's birthday was more low-key than usual. Mrs. Tilton made pigs in a blanket for supper, and Hannah made vanilla ice cream. She used twelve eggs in the recipe, and cream from our cows. She added wild strawberries right at the end. Nadine seemed more like her old self as she and I took turns churning the ice cream, cranking until our arms ached, but we forgot all about the ache when we spooned the ice cream off the dasher. If there's anything better than eating homemade strawberry ice cream with your best friend on a hot summer night, I don't know what it is.

"Let's play charades," Nadine said. We did radio shows (Nadine wanted us to do television shows, but since we didn't have a television—no one did in Vermont—Hannah and I didn't know any of those shows). For *Jack Armstrong*, first I pretended to jack up a car, and then I bent my arm and pointed to my muscle. Nadine did *The Shadow* by walking along and pointing to the ground behind her. Mrs. Tilton did *Queen for a Day* by doing a curtsy, and I thought we might die laughing when Hannah, trying to get us to say *Tarzan*, beat her chest with her fists and Mrs. Tilton yelled, "King Kong!"

Hannah suggested we do some movies ("Have you seen *The African Queen* yet?" Mrs. Tilton asked. "Bogart and Hepburn are wonderful together." "No," said Hannah, "I've been waiting for it to get here"), but Nadine was impatient to open her presents.

Nadine opened mine first. I was surprised how nervous I was when I handed it to her. I'd spent hours on it. Hannah'd had to help me with the spellings and definitions. I'd put in all my favorites. There was *grumpie* ("a pig"), *grumple* ("to feel with your fingers"—so I guess you could grumple your grumpie!), *paddock-pony* ("a tadpole"), and two dog ones: *snooker* ("someone who smells objects like a dog") and *haisk* ("to make a noise like a dog when you've got something stuck in your throat"). And *shamble-shankit* ("having crooked legs") and *glyde* ("an old horse"—which meant Dolly was a shamble-shankit glyde!), *glysterie* ("a gusty storm"), *haimart* ("belonging to home"), and my most favorite of all, *chyrme*, which was hard to pronounce (actually, it sounded most like a cat coughing up a hairball), but I thought its definition was poetry: "the mournful sound made by birds when they've gathered together before a storm."

Nadine didn't even bother looking through it, just tossed the book onto the floor and reached for another gift.

"Nadine!" Mrs. Tilton exclaimed. "What do you say?"

"Thank you," Nadine said, polite as pie, but she didn't even look at me when she said it.

Mrs. Tilton scooped up the book and leafed through the pages.

"Oh, how charming, Blue!" she said. "Some of these words are just precious!" Which made me feel better, until Nadine opened the presents from her mom. First there was a View-Master.

I'd never heard of a View-Master, but Nadine knew all about it.

"The pictures are three-dimensional," she said. She showed me how you slid the round paper discs into the viewer and pushed a little lever on the side to go on to another picture. There were discs of the Three Little Pigs, and Robin Hood, and some of the royal family (Nadine squealed when she saw those), but the ones I liked best were of Yellowstone National Park and Yosemite, the Grand Tetons, and the Grand Canyon. As I clicked through the pictures, I felt like I was glimpsing a world I would never see for real. What would it be like to actually *see* the Grand Canyon or the giant redwoods? I thought the View-Master was just about the best present anybody could get for their birthday, until Mrs. Tilton handed Nadine an envelope.

Inside were plane tickets. To London. London, England. For the coronation!

"I know it's not until next June," Mrs. Tilton told Nadine. "But I couldn't think of anything you'd like more."

I'm sure my jaw dropped. Even Nadine was speechless at first. Then she screamed so loud I thought all the windows would shatter.

I wanted to take my hand-lettered, stapled, pathetic little book of Scottish words and slink home.

Nadine clutched the tickets to her chest and danced around the room.

"I'm going to the coronation!" she squealed. "I'm going to see the queen! Can you believe it?"

No, I couldn't, but I smiled and tried to look happy for her.

"When we go through Buckingham Palace, maybe Daddy can arrange it so I could even *meet* the queen," Nadine said. "I'll have to practice my curtsy, and he'll have to bow."

Mrs. Tilton didn't answer, and a pained expression came over her face. Nadine stopped twirling to stare at her.

"What's wrong?" she asked.

"Nothing," said Mrs. Tilton. "It's just, well, Daddy won't be able to go. It'll be only the two of us."

The joy melted off Nadine's face, and I felt sorry for her. I knew what it was like to look forward to a trip and then have it pulled out from under you. But at least she was still *going* on the trip.

"Daddy's not coming with us?" Nadine said.

"No," said Mrs. Tilton.

"But . . . but it's a year away," Nadine said. "He could take vacation."

"I'm afraid not," Mrs. Tilton said. "It's simply not possible, what with his work and all. But won't it be fun, just you and me? Besides the coronation, we'll go to Piccadilly Circus, and the Tower of London, and London Bridge. We'll have a marvelous time, you'll see."

It sounded like a dream to me, and I would have traded places with Nadine right then and there, but Nadine sulked the rest of the evening. I couldn't believe she was being so bratty. She was going to England for the coronation! What more did she want? I would have been excited about a trip to *New Hampshire*.

If I could get her to see she was being ridiculous, the evening didn't have to be ruined. I waited until Hannah was in the kitchen, helping Mrs. Tilton wash the dishes, before punching Nadine lightly on the arm.

"I'll trade places with you," I said. "Do you know how lucky you are? For *my* last birthday, I got a box of crayons."

Nadine shot me a look.

"You couldn't possibly understand how I'm feeling," she snapped. "You don't even *have* a father."

I was too shocked to say anything. I stared at her, open-mouthed.

How could she have said that to me, I wondered. I was her *best friend*, or at least I thought I was. I was sorry I'd wasted my time making her that book of Scottish words—she hadn't even looked at it twice. Too bad I hadn't taken the book back and just given her a bloody nose instead.

chapter 11

"You got awfully quiet back there," Hannah said as we walked home. "You two girls have a fight or something?"

I shook my head. I was too embarrassed to tell her what Nadine had said.

Hannah wasn't fooled.

"You know, Nadine's at that age where she's going through a lot of changes," she said. "You'll be going through it yourself in another year or so. You just have to be patient with her."

I stared straight ahead. I didn't care what Hannah said. No matter what, I couldn't ever be as mean or thoughtless to Nadine as she had been to me.

"She'll be starting junior high this fall, too," Hannah said. "I'm sure that's making her nervous."

I hadn't thought about that. But if that were true, why

hadn't she told me she was nervous? Friends were supposed to tell each other things like that.

You haven't told *her* about waiting for your mama, the little voice in my head said.

"Well," Hannah said, "give it a day or two and I'm sure it'll all blow over. 'Least said, soonest mended,' I always say."

I figured Nadine would come over the next day and say she was sorry, but she didn't. She didn't come over the day after that, either. Who needed her anyway if she was going to be like that. I didn't even *want* to see her, she'd been so mean. I had other things to keep me busy, like the cat.

Hannah and I didn't know where the cat spent her days, but each morning and evening she was waiting by the barn for her food. Already she'd become part of our lives and I worried about her. I wanted to scoop her up, hug her, and tell her I'd always take care of her, but whenever I got too close, she'd run. So I squatted as close as she'd let me and talked to her while she ate. I told her things I'd never told another living soul, not even Nadine: that I was scared of clowns, and that I wanted to be a cowboy when I grew up (though after Hannah and I'd seen the movie *The Greatest Show on Earth*, I'd started thinking about being a trapeze artist), and—the biggest secret of all—that I was waiting for my real mama to come get me.

Sometimes, Hannah joined me out in the yard, where we watched the northern lights and listened to the frogs grumbling from the lake. Some nights, we saw the cat out in the orchard, hunting.

"Looks like she's planning on staying awhile," Hannah said, and my heart sang.

"What should we call her?" I asked.

Hannah thought a moment.

"Cat," she said.

I should have known better than to ask. Anybody who'd name a child Blue wasn't likely to think up anything better for a cat.

The next day, July 1, felt more like November. I put on a sweatshirt to work in the garden, but even so, I shivered. My fingers felt stiff as I picked potato bugs off the potato plants and dropped them in the can of kerosene. I remembered Miss Paisley telling us about 1816, the Year of No Summer, when they'd had snow every month of the year. No one then had known it was caused by a huge volcano the year before. I hadn't heard of any volcano blowing up, so I guessed we weren't going to have another year with no summer, but it sure felt cold. I thought about digging out my mittens, but that just seemed wrong, so I warmed my hands in my armpits instead.

Hannah was rubbing her hands, too.

"Gracious, it feels like we could get a frost tonight!" she said. "I think we'd better cover the garden." (That's the thing about living in the Northeast Kingdom—you can get a frost even in July.)

I helped Hannah carry old quilts and blankets out to the garden. I loved fall, but that didn't mean I wanted to see it coming in July! I didn't want to even think about fall yet; that would mean school starting and Nadine going home, and I wouldn't see her again till next summer.

I still hadn't quite forgiven Nadine for what she'd said about me not having a father, and I hated to admit it, but I missed her. I didn't want the whole summer to be ruined by some stupid words.

"Sometimes you just have to be the bigger person," Hannah says.

I decided that as soon as Hannah and I were done covering the garden, I'd go over and apologize (even though I hadn't done anything wrong) and make up with Nadine. So far, everything between us had been a disappointment, but that didn't mean the whole summer had to be ruined. We could still save it. I just had to remind Nadine of all the fun we'd had over the years, make her remember that I'd been her best friend long before she'd ever met her other friends. We could build a fire down by the lake, and Nadine's mom might let us make s'mores. Just the thought of Nadine and me sitting around a campfire eating s'mores made me feel better. Besides, I wanted us to make up before the July Fourth celebrations. With the parade and picnic, Nadine and I always spent the whole day at the fairgrounds and got to stay up late to watch the fireworks. It wouldn't even seem like the Fourth of July without Nadine.

Hannah and I covered the tomato and cucumber plants. As we worked, I saw Cat watching us.

"She'll be cold tonight," I said. "Maybe I could make her some sort of bed."

"She'll be warm enough in the barn," Hannah said, but when she saw me biting my lip the way I always do when I'm worried, she smiled.

"I'm sure you can find some old thing in my closet that she can sleep on," she said.

Before I left for Nadine's, I rummaged around until I found just what I wanted, a small patchwork quilt, blue with little white daisies printed on it. It was torn, and frayed at the edges, but I didn't think Cat would mind.

Hannah's mouth formed a little O when I showed it to her.

"I won't use it if you don't want me to," I said.

"No, it's not that," Hannah said. "It's just, well, that's the quilt you were wrapped in when I found you."

chapter 12

I forgot all about going to Nadine's.

"Who made the quilt?" I whispered.

"I don't know," Hannah said.

I stared at the quilt as if it could tell me who my mother was. My own mama, my *real* mama, had touched it—had maybe even made it herself, before wrapping me in it and putting me in that copper kettle.

"There wasn't a note on the quilt?" I said.

"No," said Hannah.

"You looked all around in the kettle?" I said.

"There wasn't a note," Hannah said. Her voice had a sharp edge, so I didn't ask her any more of the questions swirling inside my head.

I wondered what thoughts must have been going through my mama's head when she left me. Did she walk away without looking back, or did she stop and wonder if she was doing the right thing? Since then, had she ever thought and wondered about *me*, the way I so often wondered about *her*?

I tucked the quilt under my sweatshirt while I fed the animals, gathered eggs, and milked the cows. I sat on it while I ate supper and slept with it on my pillow, hoping it would whisper its secret to me, tell me why my mother had abandoned me.

The next day, I showed the quilt to Cat.

"This was my mama's," I told her. Finding the quilt was auspicious. Someone in the quilting club might know who had made it.

After supper, Hannah put on a sweater and picked up her basket of quilting.

"We're meeting at Ida's tonight," Hannah said. "I'll be home about ten."

"I'm going with you," I said.

Hannah eyed me suspiciously. I couldn't tell her I wanted to learn how to quilt; Hannah knew I liked sewing about as much as pounding my thumb with a hammer.

"It gets kind of lonesome here when you're gone," I said. I felt bad lying to Hannah, but I didn't want to hurt her feelings by telling her I was looking for my *real* mama.

"What do you do in the quilting club?" I asked Hannah on the way.

"Some weeks we work on our own quilts," Hannah said.

"Other times we work together on quilts for orphans or the elderly. Right now we're working on a display quilt for the celebration."

I wondered what I was getting myself into, and there were butterflies in my stomach when Mrs. Barclay met us at her door.

"Why, Blue!" she said. "I'm delighted you're joining us this evening. Finally going to learn how to quilt, are you?"

I nodded guiltily, not wanting to tell her the real reason I was there.

There were six other women besides Hannah. Except for Esther, they were all old, and they could have been sisters, all of them with gray hair and glasses and wearing aprons. They called each other by their first names—Ida, Bertha, Hortense, Mabel, Gertrude—but I called them Mrs. Barclay, Mrs. Thompson, Mrs. Potter, Mrs. Fitch, and Mrs. Appleby, except for Esther, who was the youngest in the group (besides me, of course).

Mrs. Barclay sat me next to Esther, who smiled and showed me how to make stitches so small they wouldn't show. Her fingers flew, while mine seemed big and clumsy.

I remembered all the things I hated about sewing. My thread knotted and broke, and I pricked my fingers so many times that my piece of cloth looked like it had the measles.

All around me, the women laughed and visited, chattering like a flock of starlings, and I saw it was going to be a lot harder than I thought to come right out and ask them about my mama.

The club was called Needles in a Haystack.

"Of course we were all younger, and thinner, when we picked that name," Mrs. Fitch laughed.

I thought it was a dumb name until Mrs. Appleby told me the names of some quilting clubs in nearby towns: the Nimble Thimbles, On Pins and Needles (sounded painful), Patchworks (I wasn't sure what that meant), and Sew Far, Sew Good (that one I really didn't get).

The display quilt they were working on was for the sesquicentennial and showed the story of the town's history. Some of the buildings they'd sewn into the quilt were still around, like the Congregational church, Pierce's Pharmacy, the *Monitor* office, and the town hall.

Scattered across all the tables were hundreds—no, thousands, it seemed like—of tiny pieces of cloth in every shape and color. I wondered how the women knew where all the pieces were supposed to go.

"It's like a puzzle, isn't it?" Esther said. "You have all these pieces, and each piece, by itself, is nothing, but put them together and voilà! You've made something beautiful."

The only person I'd ever heard say *voilà* before was Mrs. Tilton.

I leaned closer to see what Esther was sewing onto the quilt.

"You recognize that?" Esther asked.

I didn't want to hurt her feelings, so I hesitated.

"It looks like the Statue of Liberty," I told her.

"It *is*," she said. "Most people don't know that our town *almost* got the Statue of Liberty."

I looked at her close to see if she was kidding.

"No, it's true," she said. "Several cities and towns bid for it."

"But we didn't get it," Mrs. Thompson said. "So I don't think we should put it into the quilt."

"We were one of the towns in the running for it," said Mrs. Potter, "so I think we should include it. This quilt is about the town's history, and *almost* getting the Statue of Liberty is part of our history."

"Well, it doesn't seem quite right, putting it in," Mrs. Thompson said.

I didn't think it seemed quite right, either, but I didn't say so.

I recognized some of the people they were sewing onto the quilt, too: George Washington Henderson, Alexander Twilight, and Spencer Chamberlain. We'd learned about them in fourth grade when we were studying Vermont history. They were all people Mr. Gilpin was putting into his pageants, too.

George Washington Henderson had once been a slave, but had come to Vermont after the war, gone to college, and become a professor, minister, and school principal, teaching six subjects, including Latin, Greek, French, and German.

The thought of all those languages made my head spin; I had enough trouble just with English!

Alexander Twilight, the first black man to graduate from Middlebury College, had come here and built a huge stone school, all by himself with only the help of an ox. It was called the Old Stone House, and we'd taken a field trip there.

But my favorite story was about Spencer Chamberlain.

Spencer was famous for outrunning Runaway Pond back in 1810. It had all started when Aaron Willson needed more water to run his mill.

Just five miles away sat Long Pond, a mile long and one mile wide. If only he could get water from Long Pond, Mr. Willson thought, he'd have enough water to run a hundred mills! So he came up with a plan: he would dig a ditch from Long Pond, and the water would fill the stream and get the mill running again. But he needed help to dig that ditch. So, on Wednesday, June 6, about sixty men walked to Long Pond and started digging. What they didn't know was that right below their feet was a layer of quicksand.

That quicksand gave way under them, and all of Long Pond roared through the hole they'd dug. Mr. Willson thought of his wife, still in the mill.

"My wife!" he cried. And someone else cried, "Run, Spencer, run!"

Spencer took off running.

A wall of water forty feet high chased him down through the valley. He burst into the mill, grabbed Mrs. Willson, and dragged her far up the hillside just as the water swept the mill away.

Imagine running five miles at top speed, through thick woods, with a flood licking at your heels. Miss Paisley had said Spencer suffered from aches and pains the rest of his life. I should think so! Hannah and I lived five miles from town, and I couldn't imagine running that far with a flood chasing me. The Wright brothers hadn't interrupted Miss Paisley once when she'd told us that story, but then they loved hearing about any disaster: the *Titanic*, the San Francisco earthquake, the Chicago fire, the Johnstown flood. It made sense. The Wright brothers and disasters just seemed to go together, like macaroni and cheese.

Esther pointed out Jacob Bayley, Moses Hazen, and Timothy Hinman. They'd built the first roads here. I didn't think building roads was nearly as exciting as outrunning a runaway pond, but I didn't say so.

As I looked at the quilt, it came to me for the first time that all the famous Vermonters we'd studied were men. Not once had Miss Paisley mentioned any women. Come to think of it, we'd hardly studied any famous women, period.

"Is there something wrong?" Esther asked.

"It's just . . . ," I said. "I was just wondering . . . weren't there any famous *women* back then?"

Esther laughed.

"Of course there were," she said, "but they never get into the history books."

"Yes, it's a shame how those old stories get forgotten," said Mrs. Fitch. "Timothy Hinman's daughter was my great-great-great-grandmother, and when she was just five years old, her father left her and her brother here all winter with Indians while he went back to get the rest of the family in Connecticut. Can you imagine?"

"They were tough women back then," Mrs. Barclay agreed. "My great-great-great-grandmother walked one hundred and fifty miles through deep snow, pulling her children in a handsled, after the team of oxen starved to death." And Mrs. Appleby chimed in with, "My great-great-grandmother had to support thirteen children by herself after her husband was killed by a falling tree."

"When my great-grandfather went off to the Civil War," Mrs. Thompson said, "my great-grandmother disguised herself as a man so she'd be able to fight alongside him. My great-grandfather always said she was a better shot than he was, anyway. They only discovered she was a woman when she gave birth to my grandfather! Imagine the shock of the other soldiers when they heard that baby crying!"

Mrs. Potter told of her ancestor who'd been a doctor back when women weren't even allowed to go to college. Esther's grandmother and great-grandmother had worked all their lives for the right of women to vote, and Hannah's Scottish great-grandmother had crossed the ocean all by herself, at fifteen, to start a new life here, and her grandmother had been a nurse in the Civil War.

They all sounded like women not to be trifled with, either. Not one of them would have been scared of the Wright brothers. They would have stood up to them, not hidden in the bushes and thrown a stone.

Listening to all the stories about family, and ancestors, and recipes handed down got me to wishing again that I knew something about *my* ancestors. In third grade, when we'd studied geography, Miss Paisley had asked all of us to find out where our ancestors had come from. When she'd asked me, I'd just stared down at my feet, and Miss Paisley said, "Oh, Blue, I'm *so* sorry, I just wasn't *thinking*," which had only made it all worse. Trying to make up for it, she'd let me stick the little flag pins onto the globe, but I would have traded that for knowing who my ancestors were, and where they'd come from.

The best part of the quilting club meeting was the refreshments afterward. Mrs. Barclay served lemonade and molasses cookies, Mrs. Potter had brought brownies, and Hannah had made scones and shortbread.

Mrs. Appleby passed around pictures from a trip she'd taken to England.

"Of course, London is still terribly devastated from the war," she said, "but the surrounding countryside was glorious. We even took the train up into Scotland. You would have loved that, Hannah."

The way Hannah was studying those photos told me that she *would* have loved it. Hannah had grown up listening to stories of Scotland, and she must have dreamed about seeing it for herself someday. She probably would have, if she hadn't had me to raise. I wondered if Hannah had ever wished she hadn't taken in that squalling baby. How would her life have been different if she *hadn't* found me?

Hannah and I were all the way home before I realized I'd completely forgotten to ask about the quilt. Which meant I'd have to go to next week's meeting.

chapter 13

The week seemed unusually long, probably because I didn't have Nadine to play with. I saw her riding her bike one afternoon, and once I rode past on Dolly, but Nadine didn't even wave.

I fed the cat morning and night. She still waited until I backed away before creeping toward the bowl, but at least she wasn't running from me anymore.

"You know, when Nadine goes to the coronation, she'll probably make the queen curtsy to *her*," I told her.

The cat coughed. It could have been because she always gobbled her food too fast, but it sounded almost like a laugh to me.

The next quilting club meeting was at Mrs. Thompson's house.

"We're going to have our hands full finishing this quilt

in time," Mrs. Appleby said. "I think we'd better meet twice a week until it's finished."

The other women agreed, and everyone found a place around the quilt. I wasn't sure where to sit until Esther smiled at me and patted the seat next to her. I slid in beside her, and she handed me a needle. More pinpricked fingers, more knotted thread, but I was getting a little bit better at it.

Not that I *wanted* to get better at it. I was only there to try to get information. I sat thinking how I should bring up a conversation about the quilt—should I just show it, or ask first who'd been in the quilting group in 1941?—and was startled when I heard my name.

"I've been thinking about what Blue said last meeting," Esther said. "We *should* have put some women in the quilt."

"Well, it's too late now," said Mrs. Barclay. "There isn't *time*. We have to have this quilt *done* by August thirteenth."

"Still, we should have," Esther said. "And someone should write down all these stories of our *women* ancestors before they're lost."

"Why don't you do it, Ida?" Mrs. Fitch said. "You write your columns."

"Well, I would," Mrs. Barclay said, "but I'm going to be spending the next few weeks with my daughter and my new grandbaby."

"What about you, Hannah?" Esther asked. "You know the history better than anyone."

"Me?" Hannah said. "I'm no writer! Besides, I don't have time for that."

"Well, *someone* should," Esther said.

"I don't think the young people are even interested in hearing those stories," Mrs. Thompson said. "I know my granddaughter isn't. She'd rather listen to the radio or play records."

Mrs. Potter nodded.

"My son just got one of those newfangled televisions, and my grandchildren are already *glued* to it," she said.

"With all this new technology, they're more interested in the future, not the past," said Mrs. Appleby.

That got them to talking about how many people had died in the 1918 influenza epidemic, including Hannah's father and brother (I hadn't known that), and then Mrs. Thompson told how her mother had been the first woman in town to drive a car and she'd driven it right through the front window of Whitcher's store, and then I got so caught up in Esther's story about her cousin Marion who'd been only the third woman to hike the whole length of the Long Trail, back in 1932 (she'd even carried a pistol!), that I completely forgot about my quilt.

The third week was no better.

They started on recipes (again), then got off onto the 1927 flood (that was more interesting, hearing how high the water had gotten in town, and how many buildings and bridges had been washed away, and how a cow had been found three days later—perfectly safe—on the roof of the Municipal Building and no one could figure out how she'd gotten there). I *almost* forgot to ask about my quilt, but just as I was trying to get a word in edgeways, Mrs. Fitch jumped up and said she was sure she had a picture somewhere of that cow on the roof, and another photo of Amelia Earhart when she'd visited Vermont.

While Mrs. Fitch was rummaging through her pictures, Mrs. Potter said, "We *have* had some famous people visit here," and Hannah chimed in, "That's right. I saw Teddy Roosevelt when he came to the fairgrounds in 1912. He was campaigning, and I shook his hand, but of course, that was before women had the right to vote."

"Not only that," Mrs. Thompson said. "Tell them about the time you met Tom Thumb."

I took a good long look at Hannah. How many other things about her didn't I know, and how come I hadn't heard any of these stories before?

"It happened when I was just a little girl," Hannah began. "There was a bad storm, the wind howling, driving sleety snow against the windows. We were asleep, but Father heard someone shout. He dressed as quick as he could, took the lantern, and went to the door. There, in our yard, was a tiny coach, pulled by two little black ponies, and a man and his wife, both less than three feet tall. He introduced himself as Tom Thumb. They were on a winter tour and had come over the mountain when the storm hit. They were soaked and shivering. Mother hurried to feed them some hot tea and soup while Father took care of the horses. They slept in the very bed that Blue sleeps in now. The next morning, I thought they were playmates that Mother and Father had gotten for me, and I cried buckets when they left."

Imagine. Tom Thumb had slept in our house!

Mrs. Appleby told a story about her aunt Bertha having the hiccups for three days, which I couldn't see had anything to do with anything they'd been talking about, and then they got into a discussion about babies, and how Mrs. Potter's daughter had been in labor for seventy-two hours before having her baby, and when they got to talking about potty training, I up and decided I was going home. I mean, who wants to hear that? Especially before having refreshments!

I'd already decided I wasn't coming back, either. After three meetings, I still didn't have a clue who could have made my quilt.

I was wondering how I could sneak out (and snitch one or two of Mrs. Thompson's chocolate chip cookies without anyone noticing) when Esther pulled some pieces of fabric from her ragbag and one fluttered to the floor. It was the blue print with daisies on it.

chapter 14

I stared at Esther, trying to see myself in her face. Was she the one I'd been searching for my whole life? But before I could work up the courage to ask her, Esther stood up.

"The baby was kind of colicky when I left, so I guess I'll head home early to see how he is. See you next week," she said, and before I could utter a sound, she left.

I grabbed up the scrap of fabric and ran after her, my heart thumping against my rib cage like a trapped bird. I didn't know what I would say to her and hoped I'd come up with something clever.

When she reached the crossroads, Esther must have heard my footsteps, for she turned and gasped.

"Gracious, Blue, you startled me," she said.

"Are you my mother?" I blurted out, not being clever at all.

She looked dumbfounded, but then her face softened.

"No, child, I'm not your mother. Whatever made you think I was?"

I held up the blue print.

"This fell out of your ragbag," I said. "It's the same as the quilt I was wrapped in when Hannah found me."

Esther studied the fabric in my hand.

"Our group has been swapping quilt pieces for years," she said. "I'm afraid I don't remember who brought that cloth. I'm sorry."

I felt tears stinging my eyes.

Esther cradled my chin in her hand. She smelled of lavender.

"I'm not your mother," she said, tenderly, "but I wish I were. I'd love a daughter like you."

I turned and stumbled toward home. I was starting to realize that finding out about my mama was going to be a lot like making a quilt: one piece at a time.

"Why'd you leave the meeting in such a hurry?" Hannah wanted to know.

I was careful not to look her in the eyes; Hannah could spot a fib from fifty yards.

"Esther dropped something out of her bag," I said, and left it at that. It was the truth.

Just not the *whole* truth.

Over the next couple of days, my deliveries took longer than usual. At every door, I studied the face of the woman who answered it and thought, Could *she* be my mother? I showed each one of them the print fabric and asked if they recognized it. They all shook their heads.

I had a dozen cookies to leave at Mrs. Wheaton's. She loved Hannah's molasses cookies and ordered a dozen every week. She was old enough to be my great-grandmother, so I was pretty sure she wasn't my mother. Mrs. Wheaton hadn't been at the quilting club meeting any of the nights I was there, either, so I was wondering whether to even show her the fabric when she noticed it sticking out of my pocket.

"That looks like one of Peddler Jenny's prints," she said.

I looked at her blankly.

"Peddler Jenny," Mrs. Wheaton repeated. "She came by every summer, selling needles, thread, fabrics, that sort of thing. Some of her cloth came from Boston. It was too expensive for our wallets, but the summer people who came to our group would buy it and bring it to share with us. We loved swapping our pretty feed sacks for those beautiful prints."

"What happened to Peddler Jenny?" I asked.

"I don't know, Blue," Mrs. Wheaton said. "She just stopped coming around."

I had a gooseberry pie and a dozen cookies for Mrs. Tilton. Nadine came to the door with her mom, stuck her nose in the air, and flounced back inside, but I hardly noticed. I didn't have time to worry about her. Mrs. Wheaton had given me a new lead to follow.

At supper, Hannah set a bowl of mashed potatoes in front of me.

"Do you remember a woman peddler that used to come around here?" I asked, trying to sound casual.

"Jenny?" Hannah said. "Sure. She came through every summer, pushing an old baby carriage piled with goods. We always tried to buy something from her, being that she had a no-account husband and nine children."

I choked on a spoonful of potato. Nine children! Where would I have fit in there?

Hannah thumped me on the back.

"Where'd she live?" I asked as soon as I could speak.

"I think she lived on the road, poor thing," Hannah said. "All those children just got dragged from pillar to post."

"Do you know what happened to her?" I asked.

"No," said Hannah. "She just stopped coming around."

"*When* did she stop coming around?" I asked.

"Well, let's see," Hannah said, pausing to think. "I'm not sure I can recollect, but seems to me it was right around when the war started."

The same time I was left in Hannah's copper kettle.

- - -✕✕✕- -

chapter 15

- -✕✕- - - - - -

Dreams of driving off with my mother in a brand-new 1952 DeSoto went up in smoke. If Peddler Jenny was my mama, I'd be helping her push an old baby carriage, and instead of ice cream and candy every day, we'd probably be eating roadside weeds.

I still wanted to find her, to see if she really *was* the person who'd left me behind. But how could I track her down, I wondered. I'd have to act like a detective, like Humphrey Bogart in *The Maltese Falcon*. Or Nancy Drew. I could call it *The Case of the Disappearing Peddler*.

Raleigh was sweeping when I got to the *Monitor*.

"Blue True," he said.

Mr. Gilpin looked up when I walked into his office. He was working at his desk, a cigar clamped between his teeth.

He was scowling, like he had indigestion or something. He looked, well, cantankerous.

"It's not the night we make up the paper, so you can't be here with our usual delivery," he said. "Too bad. I could use one of Hannah's doughnuts right about now."

He waved a hand at the stack of papers on his desk. "I've just finished the scene for the signing of the town charter, in 1802. Most folks don't know John Paul Jones was one of the original grantees of the town. And did you know that Lafayette visited here? He actually got poor old Colonel Barton released from debtors' prison."

If he was talking famous people, I wondered if Mr. Gilpin knew about Mrs. Fitch seeing Amelia Earhart, or that Hannah had shaken Teddy Roosevelt's hand.

"I was thinking of asking Roy Allard to play Colonel Barton," Mr. Gilpin went on. "I'd get a kick out of slapping him in jail, even if it was just for fun."

Mr. Allard was the editor of the *Caledonia Record*. He'd been at the *Monitor* a few times when I'd delivered doughnuts, and every time, he and Mr. Gilpin had been arguing about something or other. I took it that they didn't like each other much.

"Could I look at some of your old newspapers?" I asked.

"You mean back issues?" Mr. Gilpin said. "They're stored down cellar. What did you want to look up?"

I hadn't expected to have to give a reason, and my

stomach churned. I couldn't tell him I was looking for my mama; he'd be sure to tell Hannah. Then I heard the paper in my pocket crinkle.

"Um . . . I—I'm interested in the circus," I stammered.

"You mean that circus that came through about five years ago?" Mr. Gilpin asked, and I nodded.

"There were some stolen animals—" I started to say, but Mr. Gilpin interrupted me.

"Never did find out what happened to those animals, poor things," he said. "They'd had a hard life in that circus, weren't very well taken care of from the looks of them. That's why we didn't give the owners permission to come back. But you're welcome to look up the story on it in our back issues. Anything else?"

"Um . . . I'd also like to look up the papers for 1941," I told him. "I'm doing a project for school." Good thing Mr. Gilpin didn't know me that well, or he would have *known* I would never waste part of summer vacation doing a project for school.

"Oh, Pearl Harbor," Mr. Gilpin said. "You want the papers just for December?"

I swallowed.

"No, I'd like to see them from the summer, too."

"Oh, how things were here on the home front before we entered the war," he said. Mr. Gilpin was doing a whole lot of assuming, but that was fine by me. Meant I didn't have to do so much lying.

"We've got a lot of veterans around you could interview for your project, give you firsthand accounts."

"Thanks, Mr. Gilpin, maybe I will," I said. "Right now, I'm just looking up information."

"Raleigh," Mr. Gilpin called. "Show Blue where the back issues are."

I followed Raleigh down the narrow stairs and to the back room, where stacks of old newspapers were piled all the way to the ceiling. My heart sank. This was going to be harder than I thought.

Raleigh pulled a lemon drop from his pocket. It looked fuzzy, with all the lint stuck to it. He held it out to me.

"No thanks," I said, and Raleigh popped the lemon drop into his mouth, lint and all. I saw the corner of a baseball card sticking out of his pocket. I wondered if it was one I already had. Did Raleigh collect baseball cards, too? Before I could ask him, he turned and went back upstairs.

I found the pile of 1941 papers. They were yellow and musty-smelling. I stood on a chair so I could reach the top of the stack, and a cloud of dust made me sneeze. I pulled off the top paper. It was so brittle that some of the edges flaked off when I opened it.

Mrs. Barclay wrote a weekly column on everyone's comings and goings. Busybodying, Hannah would have called it—she hated gossip—but those columns just might give me a clue to my mother.

I dug through the papers and found the one for

Thursday, December 11, the first issue that would have come out after December 7. Most of the news dealt with Pearl Harbor, of course, but the very first item in Mrs. Barclay's column caught my eye.

> Hannah Spooner got the surprise of her life Sunday morning when she found a baby in the copper kettle out in her front yard. The baby weighs only three pounds but is doing well, Hannah reports.

Hannah hadn't ever told me I weighed only three pounds. I must have been born early. Which meant folks might not have even been able to *tell* my mama was going to have a baby just by looking at her. She might have just looked like she'd eaten a big Thanksgiving dinner.

I went back through all the papers for 1941 and found Peddler Jenny mentioned three times—"Peddler Jenny was in the area on Wednesday," that sort of thing—but the October 24 column finally gave me a clue.

> We extend our sympathies to Peddler Jenny on the death of her husband. The service was held in Barre.

Had Peddler Jenny been so upset over the death of her husband, and scared, wondering how she was going to feed another child on top of the nine she already had, that she'd left me in Hannah's kettle? Maybe I could find some answers in Barre, people who'd known her and might know where she'd gone. But Barre was over fifty miles away. I couldn't exactly ask Hannah to drive me there. I'd have to take a train or a bus.

I sighed. It was going to take money to travel around looking for my mama, and I didn't have any. Maybe I could get Nadine's mom to pay me for cleaning out their attic. Maybe Mr. Gilpin would give me a paper route. I didn't have a bike, but I could deliver papers on Dolly, along with my other deliveries.

"Blue!" Mr. Gilpin called down the stairs. "I'll be closing up soon."

Had that much time passed already? Hannah was going to be wondering where I was. There'd be questions, and I'd have to make up some answers.

I shoved the papers back into a pile and scrambled up the stairs.

"Find what you were looking for?" Mr. Gilpin asked.

I nodded, my face feeling extra warm.

"You know, I never did believe those animals were stolen," Mr. Gilpin said. "I think the operators of that circus were con artists and just said the animals were stolen to try to cheat us out of some money."

Oh.

"Speaking of animals, I should have sent you home

earlier," Mr. Gilpin said. "That old horse might have a hard time seeing, now that it's twilight. You'll need the fireflies to light your way home."

What was that word Nadine had used, the one about fireflies and things that happen at twilight? Oh yes, *cre-PUS-cu-lar*.

"What did you say?" Mr. Gilpin said.

I ducked my head with embarrassment. Had I said that out loud?

"Crepuscular," I said. "Fireflies are crepuscular insects, but it's not a very pretty word. Hannah calls the evening gloaming, but that's not pretty, either. I think *twilight* sounds better."

Mr. Gilpin stared at me, and I wished the earth would just swallow me whole. What was the matter with me, rattling on about twilight and fireflies? Mr. Gilpin was going to think I was missing some marbles.

The corner of Mr. Gilpin's mouth curled up into a smile.

"How'd you like a job, kid?" he asked.

I wasn't sure I'd heard right.

"Ida Barclay's going to be away right up until the celebration, visiting her daughter," Mr. Gilpin went on. "I need someone to write her column while she's gone. You want the job?"

Working at the newspaper seemed like a way I

might be able to find out more information about my
mama.

So I rode home as the newest reporter for the *Monitor*,
all because of *crepuscular*.

Reader's Digest was right. It *did* pay to increase your
word power.

chapter 16

First thing I did when I got home was tell Cat about my new job.

"Maybe I'll be a writer instead of a cowboy," I told her.

Cat finished off the milk in the bowl and cleaned herself. I guess the newspaper business didn't interest her that much, but I was excited. I was going to be a reporter, like Lois Lane!

That excitement lasted until the next morning, when it was replaced with panic. What did I know about writing a newspaper column? I couldn't spell worth beans, and now I'd be a laughingstock in town. People would point and whisper behind my back.

I rode into town thinking I'd tell Mr. Gilpin that I'd made a terrible mistake, that I really didn't want to write the column, but somewhere between my house and the *Monitor*, I lost my nerve and ended up bringing home some of

Mrs. Barclay's columns that Mr. Gilpin pushed on me to read so I'd know what I was supposed to write.

I made another decision, on the way home, one I was determined to keep. I was going to ask Nadine for help. She wrote for her school newspaper; she'd know what to do. No matter what she'd said to me, it was time to make up, and if Nadine wouldn't make the first move, then I'd have to. All I had to do was remind Nadine how much fun we'd had over the years, how much fun we could *still* have this summer. We'd been friends for too long to let it all go to waste.

My determination went up in smoke when I climbed the steps to Nadine's camp. I felt more like I was making my way to the guillotine. My knees wobbled as I knocked on the door (which shows how nervous I was, because in all the years Nadine and I had known each other, we never knocked on each other's door—we always just burst in on each other, like family).

Nadine answered the door, and her eyes narrowed. I jumped in, quick, before she could slam the door in my face.

"I'm a reporter for the *Monitor* now," I told her. "I thought you could give me some advice about my column." If there was one thing Nadine liked, it was giving advice. But I didn't tell her I hoped this job was also going to help me find my mother.

Nadine seemed to take forever deciding.

"Okay, you can come in," Nadine said, and I followed her up to her room.

I dumped the papers on Nadine's bed.

"You know, it's just a gossip column," she said, all hoity-toity. "It's not like you're a *real* reporter."

I knew she was only saying all that because she was jealous Mr. Gilpin hadn't picked *her* to write the column, but it still made me mad. Here I was, being nice to her, and she kept on being mean. Why was I always the one who had to apologize, even when it wasn't my fault? I picked up one of the papers and blinked fast so Nadine wouldn't see the tears in my eyes.

"Why's it even called the *Monitor*?" Nadine asked. "Seems like a funny name for a newspaper."

I shrugged, wishing I hadn't bothered to come over in the first place.

"Of course, it isn't even a *real* newspaper," Nadine went on. "Not like the *New York Times*. When we lived in New York, Daddy always read the *New York Times*. Now he reads the *Washington Post*, but he still subscribes to the *New York Times* too."

I ignored her while I flipped through the pages for Mrs. Barclay's column.

"It's right there, on the back," Nadine said, snatching the paper out of my hands. If there was one thing Nadine hated, it was being ignored.

Nadine scanned the column and snorted.

"I told you!" she said, rolling her eyes. "This isn't *news*. This column could put people to sleep!"

I glared at her and snatched the paper back. I wanted to smack Nadine, but reading the column, I saw she was right.

> Miss Cynthia Ryder remains about the same.

What did that mean? I wondered. Remains the same as what?

> Miss Claire Boisvert has returned to her home in Quebec after visiting with her aunt.
>
> Mr. Harley Thompson has been having problems with a hernia and is confined to bed.

I saw two problems right off. First, I sure didn't want to be writing about things like hernias! Second, how was I going to find the news? Mrs. Barclay just called folks to ask them about their comings and goings and family news, but the thought of calling grown-ups to ask them about their business made my stomach ache. Besides, we didn't have a telephone. That left interviewing them in person, but just the idea made me break into a sweat. I didn't think I could bear it if Mrs. Thompson started talking about her husband's hernia.

"I'm pretty sure the *New York Times* doesn't report on people's hernias," Nadine said.

As mad as I was at her, I was pretty sure she was right.

"Okay," Nadine said. "You obviously need my help." I didn't tell her that instead of helping, she was just making me more nervous. Thinking about being nervous reminded me what Hannah had said.

"Are you nervous about starting junior high this fall?" I asked her.

"Of course not," Nadine said, tossing her head. "There's nothing to be nervous about." And then I knew she *was*.

"Well, I know I'll be nervous when I start junior high," I said.

Nadine chewed on her lip, and for a moment, I thought she was going to confide in me, but then she changed her mind.

"It's not like you have to change schools, the way I do," she declared. "You'll still all just be in that one-room schoolhouse."

What did that have to do with anything? I wondered. But instead of asking her, I decided just to go home and read through the rest of the columns.

Hannah wasn't too keen on me taking the job ("You know I don't hold with spreading gossip," she said), but when she saw how nervous I was, her face softened.

"All you have to do is just visit with folks when you make your deliveries," she said. "Ask them how they are, then sit back and listen. Being a good reporter is mostly about being a good listener."

That sounded simple enough, but still, when I rode up to Mrs. Gallagher's door the next afternoon, I felt like I had about a hundred of those crepuscular fireflies in my stomach. Maybe I wasn't cut out to be a reporter after all.

Mrs. Gallagher answered the door. I could hear loud moans coming from inside the house. Sounded like a cow bellowing.

Mrs. Gallagher gave a wave of her hand.

"Oh, that's Roger," she said. "Painful gas, don't you know. He was playing in the old-timers game at the ball field and ate three chili dogs! Serves him right, I say."

This was worse than hearing about Mr. Thompson's hernia. I was sure Mr. Gallagher wouldn't want me reporting on his gas pains. I mean, would you want the whole town knowing that?

The next day was Sunday. Hannah said I ought to catch people at church and interview them. All through the service, I felt nervous as a long-tailed cat in a room full of rocking chairs, swinging my legs and chewing my lip, wondering who I should interview, and what questions I should ask. A hundred times I wished I hadn't agreed to write Mrs. Barclay's column. What was I thinking?

Folks clustered in little groups on the church lawn after the service, visiting. Hannah pulled a little notebook and pencil from her purse. She handed them to me and gave me a nudge.

"Go on," she said, but when I shook my head, she strode right out into the middle of the lawn.

"Blue's writing Ida's column while she's away," Hannah announced in a loud voice, "and she'd really appreciate whatever news you could tell her."

I wanted the ground to open up and swallow me, I was so embarrassed, but folks did come over to speak to me, and I filled up two pages of Hannah's little notebook.

That afternoon, instead of going to the ball field, I worked at writing the column.

By chore time, this is what I ended up with:

> Mrs. Hortense Potter caught her hand in her wringer washer.
>
> Mr. Clem Hazelton is looking for the person who lost a carburetor cap in his yard.
>
> Mrs. Bertha Thompson has some tripe she's willing to give away.
>
> Mrs. Ernestine Wilkins is overrun with beet greens and string beans and says come help yourself.
>
> Mr. Ned Butler reports a missing sheep.

I was sure Nadine would roll her eyes at what I'd written, so I didn't even show it to her, and Mr. Gilpin made me rewrite it seven times before he said it was acceptable (I'd had to look through most of the C section of his dictionary to find out how to spell *carburetor*), but Thursday morning, when the paper came out and I saw my name, Blue Spooner, in print, something opened in my chest, like a flower opening to the sun.

I watched across the supper table, my hands sweaty, as Hannah read my column. She refolded the paper and set it down beside her plate. The corners of her mouth turned up in a smile.

"Ida just might find herself out of a job when she gets back," Hannah said.

chapter 17

I carried the paper out when I fed Cat, and read my column to her while she ate, and went to bed with a nice warm glow.

But the next morning, I found out a weekly column is a lot more work than it looks. I realized I couldn't just sit back and enjoy what I'd written; I had to start right away working on *next* week's column. I had to go back and ask the same folks that I'd just talked to if they had any *new* news (most of them didn't), and even when I found something interesting, Mr. Gilpin wasn't happy with how I'd written it, and would make me keep working on it until I just wanted to heave the whole thing out the window. But that feeling changed when Mr. Gilpin handed me my first paycheck, made out in my name, for $3.27. I couldn't spend it—I had to put it in the college fund jar—but it still felt sweet, and it spurred me on.

On my deliveries, Mr. Appleby told me his radio was on

the blink, and Mrs. Appleby told me how her sister had made herself a new hat (I didn't think either of those things was interesting enough to put in my column), and I was only half listening when Mrs. Gray launched into a story about her daughter. What *did* get my attention was when she said she wouldn't need any of her regular deliveries the next week because she'd be visiting her daughter in Montpelier.

Montpelier was only a few miles from Barre.

I rode on, trying to figure out a way I could ask Mrs. Gray if I could go along with her, and I was still thinking when I dropped off Mr. Hazelton's delivery of three loaves of bread and a dozen filled cookies.

I liked Mr. Hazelton. He'd been a cowboy out west ("Came east with a load of horses, liked the country, and stayed," he'd told me once), and it was his stories of being a cowboy that had made me want to be a cowboy, too. He showed me how to twirl a lariat, and I'd practiced lassoing the cows until Hannah put a stop to it.

"You're making them so nervous they're giving less milk," she'd said.

Mr. Hazelton bit into one of the cookies.

"Hannah's cookies taste just like the ones my grandmother used to make," he said. I nodded, not really listening. There *had* to be a way I could get to Barre.

"Say, did Ned ever find that missing sheep?" Mr. Hazelton asked.

"I don't think so," I said.

"Just wondered," Mr. Hazelton said, "because Raymond Lapointe's got a calf missing as well. It broke its leg, so he was going to ship it to the slaughterhouse, but it up and disappeared. You might want to put that in your column."

I didn't want to just be reporting on missing animals—I wasn't writing a lost and found column!—but I wrote it down anyway.

Mr. Hazelton scratched his head.

"You know, it sure is strange how a calf with a broken leg could just up and disappear. Maybe Ned's sheep didn't wander off on its own, either."

"You mean, you think someone *stole* them?" I asked.

"Well, that calf couldn't have walked off on its own now, could it?" Mr. Hazelton said.

I rode along, feeling more excited by the minute. Here was my chance! If someone had stolen the animals, that made it a real news story. If I could find out who'd done it, I could write up an article for the newspaper, just like a *real* reporter. I might even be able to find out who'd stolen the circus animals, too. It wasn't hard thinking up two possible suspects.

The Wright brothers.

I'd have to get proof—catch the Wright brothers with the animals—but it'd be better if I had some help. I sure didn't want to be snooping around the Wright farm all by myself. My stomach felt wobbly even *thinking* about that,

but reporters sometimes had to put themselves in danger-
ous situations. And it wouldn't seem quite so scary if I had
Nadine helping me. She and I could be a team, like the
Hardy Boys.

I was so wrapped up in thinking of all the different mys-
teries we could solve that I didn't even notice I was at Mrs.
Wells's house until I saw her on her porch waving an envelope at me. My heart sank. I didn't want to get caught listening to a long, boring story. I had a case to solve!

"Thought you might like an extra copy of your column
for your scrapbook," Mrs. Wells said.

I didn't tell Mrs. Wells that I didn't have a scrapbook,
and I didn't tell her that Mrs. Appleby, Esther, Mrs. Thompson, and Mr. Hazelton had *all* given me extra copies of my
column.

"Thank you, Mrs. Wells," I said. That was nice of her,
saving my column for me, and I felt sorry I'd complained so
much about her. Hannah was right: she was just lonely.

"It's quite the responsibility, isn't it, having to write a
weekly column?" Mrs. Wells said. I nodded, feeling more
kindly toward her by the minute.

Mrs. Wells gripped my arm.

"Well, you come in and sit down and I'll tell you all
about my sister's operation on her toe."

That made me even more determined to be a reporter.
Mr. Gilpin didn't have to sit around listening to stories
about hernias, toe operations, or new hats! He was forever

rushing off to fires, or accidents, or interviews with important people, and he and Mr. Allard were always trying to "scoop" each other on those stories. It made me think that if I could get proof it was the Wright brothers who'd stolen the missing animals, I could scoop *them*. My article might even make the front page!

Maybe I *ought* to start keeping a scrapbook to hold my columns and the articles I was going to write.

Mr. Gilpin let me type up my columns on his typewriter. When he first sat me in front of it, with its gleaming gold letters spelling out OLIVETTI staring back at me, I was scared to touch it, but he showed me how to put the paper in and how to push the lever on the return carriage when I got to the end of a line (I loved hearing that little bell!). I had to punch the keys with my fingers, but I liked watching the way the little arms would swing up and smack the paper to print the letters. Except when I made mistakes. Then I had to go back, put in a new piece of paper, and start all over again.

I was forever having to look up spellings, too, in the huge dictionary on Mr. Gilpin's desk. I'd never known anyone to read a dictionary the way Mr. Gilpin did; he liked words even more than Nadine did.

While I worked on my columns, Mr. Gilpin worked more on writing his pageants for the sesquicentennial celebration.

"I'm working on the one about Mr. Webster right now,"

Mr. Gilpin said. When he saw that I didn't know who Mr. Webster was, he pointed to a photograph on the wall beside one of the file cabinets. I'd never noticed the picture before.

"Mr. Ellery Webster, founder of the *Monitor*," Mr. Gilpin said. "He was with the Eleventh Vermont in the Civil War. Got captured, sent to Andersonville Prison in Georgia, and came home weighing just seventy pounds. He was a hero, but he said the ones who didn't come back were the real heroes."

I leaned in to get a closer look at Mr. Webster.

"Times like that test a man, bring out his true colors," Mr. Gilpin said.

I didn't know what Mr. Gilpin was talking about, but from the look in Mr. Webster's eyes, you could tell he'd been through some awful times.

"Mr. Webster wrote some fine articles about his experiences," Mr. Gilpin said. "You might want to look them up sometime, in the back issues. He had a way with words."

I wondered if that was Mr. Gilpin's nice way of saying I *didn't* have a way with words.

After I finished typing up my column, Mr. Gilpin decided I needed a tour of the building to see how the *Monitor* was produced. He showed me the Linotype machine, which produced a line of type that was then placed in forms that went on the press to print the paper. He gave it a loving pat, as if it were an old horse.

"This machine revolutionized typesetting," he said. "Before this, we had to set type all by hand, one letter at a time. It took hours."

Downstairs, besides all the stacks of old newspapers, was the big flatbed press that printed the paper.

"I started out as a printer's devil, just like Raleigh," Mr. Gilpin said. "Mr. Jacobs was the owner and editor then, and he let me set type, and even run the press. It was the most fascinating thing I'd ever done, and I knew then that I'd found my calling, what I wanted to do with my life."

I wondered what that would feel like, to be so sure of what you wanted to do with your life. I was still trying to decide between cowboy and trapeze artist.

"I've had a rich, rewarding life," Mr. Gilpin said. "But I've always regretted that I didn't get my high school diploma."

I think my jaw must have dropped a little. Mr. Gilpin, the smartest person I knew, hadn't gone to college!

"It's made me work harder," Mr. Gilpin went on. "Roy Allard went to Harvard, and you can be sure there's not a day goes by that he doesn't remind me of that, and that he's going to do his best to beat me to every story—to get there first, and to report on it better."

I didn't tell Mr. Gilpin that that's what I was going to do with my story on the missing animals. Wouldn't Mr. Gilpin and Mr. Allard be surprised when I scooped *both* of them!

chapter 18

Mr. Gilpin leaned back in his chair.

"There, I've finished," he announced. "We'll set Saturday as the first rehearsal for the pageant."

He told me which events he'd chosen for the re-enactments and let me read what he'd written. He had Rogers's Rangers fleeing back to Vermont after they'd attacked an Abenaki village in Quebec with the Abenakis in hot pursuit; there was the signing of the town charter in 1802, the War of 1812, and the Embargo Act, where Thomas Jefferson had declared it illegal to trade with the English in Canada, so smuggling became common. The smuggling caused many skirmishes between town officials and the smugglers. In one of those skirmishes, in 1814, John Ware was shot in the leg and had to have it amputated.

"I'm going to play John Ware myself," Mr. Gilpin said

with a grin. "I'm perfect for the role. I'll just have to make sure that the leg Doc saws off is my *wooden* leg!"

"Who's going to play the smugglers?" I asked.

Mr. Gilpin chewed his lip.

"Well, I was thinking of the Wright brothers," he said, "but knowing them, I'm worried they might just show up with a *real* gun."

I thought Mr. Gilpin was smart to worry about that.

"Well," I said, "if you *did* put them in, you could throw them in jail and then, accidentally on purpose, lose the key."

Mr. Gilpin slapped his wooden leg and roared with laughter.

"By golly, that's a dandy idea," he said. "I just might do that."

For the reenactment of Runaway Pond, Mr. Gilpin was having Raleigh play Spencer Chamberlain.

"In high school, Raleigh was the fastest runner in the Kingdom," Mr. Gilpin said.

With his long legs, I could imagine that Raleigh'd always been fast. What I couldn't imagine was that Raleigh had ever gone to high school.

"With the right coaching, Raleigh could have been in the Olympics," Mr. Gilpin said. "He had real potential before . . . well, before his accident."

I wanted to ask Mr. Gilpin about Raleigh's accident, but it didn't seem right, somehow. It was hard to imagine

Raleigh *before.* I'd only known him *after.* It showed how fast things could change. One minute you're a track star, your whole life ahead of you, and the next, you've got a dent in your head, and the only words you can say are *Blue True* and *baby.*

"Mind you, he's still fast," Mr. Gilpin said. "Well, he would be, wouldn't he?" And I looked at him blankly, wondering what he was talking about.

"Stands to reason he'd be fast," Mr. Gilpin repeated. "Raleigh is Spencer Chamberlain's great-great-great-grandson."

Imagine that.

"Will any of Raleigh's family be at the pageant to watch him?" I asked. I was curious to see what Raleigh's family looked like.

Mr. Gilpin shook his head.

"Raleigh doesn't have family," Mr. Gilpin said. "A second wave of influenza passed through here in 1920, and both of Raleigh's parents died from it. Raleigh had just been born, so he was sent off to live with his grandmother, but she died when he was sixteen, so he came back to live on the old homeplace. He's been on his own ever since."

So Raleigh and I did have some things in common: he never got to know his mother or father, either.

"Have you ever been to his house?" I asked, thinking of the stories all the kids at school had made up about him.

119

"Not since his folks lived there," said Mr. Gilpin. "Then, when the road and bridge to that place washed out in the '27 flood, the town never did build them back, didn't seem to be a need, with no one living there. Now it's just too hard a place to get to, especially for a man with one leg. But Raleigh seems to like the solitude out there. I imagine he feels safer."

Harder for the Wright brothers to get out there is what I imagined Mr. Gilpin meant.

Mr. Gilpin stood up.

"I'll run off copies of these pageant scripts and tell everyone about the rehearsal," he said. "If we meet up at the lake at ten o'clock, that should be good, don't you think?" He was out the door before I could even answer. Mr. Gilpin might not feel he was up to walking to Raleigh's place, but he still moved pretty fast for a man with just one leg.

I was happy for him when I saw Saturday dawn bright and cloudless, not a hint of rain. A perfect day for the rehearsal.

I didn't have any trouble getting Nadine to come along (I think she was hoping Mr. Gilpin would give her a part in the pageant), and the trip to town, both of us riding Dolly, went quickly. Nadine seemed like her old self, mostly, until we came to the lake and she saw Raleigh. She wrinkled her nose.

"What's he doing here?" she asked.

"He's playing Spencer Chamberlain," I told her.

"I hope it isn't a *speaking* part," Nadine said, which I thought was mean.

"We're going to start with the Runaway Pond pageant," Mr. Gilpin announced.

Mr. Gilpin had painted waves onto large pieces of cardboard and attached them to the side of a wagon, so that the two older Trombley boys could pull the wagon and it would look like the waves were chasing Raleigh as he ran.

Mr. Gilpin had also made a cardboard box to look like a mill. That's where I'd be, as Mrs. Willson, for Raleigh to pull me out and rescue me, but Mr. Gilpin was just going over our lines when the Wright brothers showed up. Dennis had a burlap bag slung over his shoulder, and I noticed he set it down by the Indian village that was to be used for the Rogers's Raid pageant. We'd be rehearsing that later. I was going to play an Abenaki woman in that one.

Mr. Gilpin went over where we were all supposed to stand during the pageant, and I was trying to pay attention, but I got distracted when I saw Nadine had gone over to the Indian village and was talking to the Wright brothers. Nadine didn't really know them, and I'd warned her plenty to stay away from them, so I wondered what they could be talking about, but Mr. Gilpin was ready to start, so I walked down to the "mill," where I was supposed to be. Nadine came with me. She smirked when she saw the cardboard mill.

"I knew this was an *amateur* production," she said, "but *really.*"

I thought Mr. Gilpin had done a good job constructing the mill, but I didn't say so.

Mr. Gilpin was pointing out to Raleigh where he was supposed to run when he was interrupted by Wesley and Dennis.

"Run, run!" they screamed. "Don't let Raleigh bite you! He's got rabies!" They doubled over with laughter.

I looked at Nadine. She turned her head away, but not before I saw her face redden.

"That's enough!" Mr. Gilpin yelled. "Dennis, Wesley, not another word out of you."

I turned to Nadine.

"Why would you have told them that?" I asked.

"Why, was I not supposed to?" Nadine said, all innocent. "I didn't know it was a secret. You should have told me."

I glared at her, but I felt sick. She was right. It *was* my fault. She shouldn't have told the Wright brothers, and they *were* being awful, the way they were picking on Raleigh, but they never would have known if *I* hadn't told Nadine.

Things went downhill from there. Dennis set off some fireworks, which spooked Dolly, and she took off, tearing through the Indian village that Mr. Gilpin had set up for the Rogers's Raid pageant, scattering Trombleys every which way. Luckily, she didn't trample anybody, but just as Mr. Gilpin and Hannah were trying to round the Trombleys back up, Mr. Hazelton, playing one of Rogers's Rangers, picked up the burlap bag that Dennis had brought and threw it over his shoulder. The bag was to be used for hauling away the gold and silver that the rangers loot from the Indian village and carry back to Vermont.

A funny look came over Mr. Hazelton's face, and he set the bag down. Out from the bag marched a skunk. A very angry-looking skunk. It took one look at all of us, turned, and lifted its tail. That sent everyone scattering as well.

Mr. Gilpin looked almost as mad as that skunk, and I was figuring that right about then he was wishing he could dispatch the Wright brothers, too. I felt bad for him. His rehearsal had turned into a disaster, which was just what the Wright brothers had wanted.

chapter 19

After that first rehearsal, we all wondered if Mr. Gilpin would just cancel the whole shebang, but he surprised us. He stood up in church the next day and announced that he was holding another rehearsal that afternoon.

We all looked at each other, wondering what Mr. Gilpin could be *thinking*, and wondering if everyone would be scared off by the Wright brothers, but by two o'clock, over a hundred townspeople had shown up at the lake, some to rehearse, but others just to see what the Wright brothers would do.

"Gives you a sinking feeling in the pit of your stomach, doesn't it?" Mrs. Thompson said, and Mr. Hazelton nodded.

"It's like driving by a car wreck. You just can't help but look," he said.

So imagine everyone's surprise when Mr. Gilpin showed up *with* the Wright brothers!

"Dennis and Wesley are going to play the smugglers," Mr. Gilpin said. "Depending on how they do, I'd also like them to play some of the Indians that Rogers's Rangers attack."

Before, I'd wanted to play one of Rogers's Rangers, but now I was glad I wasn't. One thing about Dennis and Wesley, pageant or no pageant, you *knew* they'd attack back.

"Have you lost your mind?" Hannah asked Mr. Gilpin.

"If you can't beat them, join them," Mr. Gilpin said. "Or at least get them to join you. You know that old saying, 'Keep your friends close and your enemies closer.'"

"I hope you know what you're doing," Hannah said.

"Me too," said Mr. Gilpin.

We were all on pins and needles wondering what mischief the Wright brothers would get into, but to everyone's amazement (and except for Dennis almost putting out Pierre Trombley's eye with an arrow), the rehearsal went off with hardly a hitch.

Maybe Mr. Gilpin had had the right idea after all, but I wasn't convinced. Dennis and Wesley hadn't turned over new leaves all of a sudden. I smelled a rat; they were up to something. Maybe I'd be able to find out just what they were up to when I spied on them. It was time I figured out when, and how, I was going to carry out my spying expedition.

Monday morning, Hannah and I were still talking about the rehearsal—and I was thinking about how I could sneak away to start spying—as we finished up milking. I turned the cows back out while Hannah washed up the milk pails and cream separator, then I followed her into the house for breakfast. Maybe, on my deliveries, I could swing by the Wright place and start snooping around. There was a pair of old army binoculars up in the attic; if I took those, I might be able to spot the animals at the Wrights' without having to get so close.

Hannah dished up oatmeal and began slicing a loaf of bread.

"I hardly got a drop from Daisy this morning," I told Hannah.

"I know, she's drying up," Hannah said. "And I'm afraid she's too old to have another calf."

The spoon stopped halfway to my mouth. I knew what that meant. Cows only produce milk after they've had a calf, and if a cow can't produce milk, she's good for just one thing.

Meat.

The last time Hannah had butchered a cow, Beulah, I'd been too young to remember it. All the cows we had now, how many hundreds of times had I rested my head against them as I milked, talked to them, sung to them? I *knew* them. Peony was partial to apples, while Tulip liked carrots. Rose had to be the first one in the barn or she got snippety. Daffodil enjoyed Christmas songs like "Jingle Bells" and "Santa Claus Is Coming to Town," while Chrysanthemum preferred hymns. Iris hated thunderstorms and dogs. And Daisy, she liked to be scratched behind her ears.

Poor Daisy. I knew farmers couldn't afford to keep cows as pets, but I didn't want her turned into hamburger and pot roasts.

Hannah took off her apron and set it on the counter.

"Those peas and beans are going to get by us if we don't can them this afternoon," Hannah said. "I need to slip into town for a new seal for the pressure cooker, but while I'm gone, you can start bringing up the jars."

I hated canning time. Hannah had hundreds of glass canning jars in the cellar that every year had to be carried up, washed in hot, soapy water, and then carried back down to put on the shelves once she'd filled them. She had so many jars that after she filled all the shelves, she lined both sides of the stairs with them as well.

"That's an accident waiting to happen," Mr. Gilpin told her. "Get Raleigh to build you some more shelves."

"I can build my own shelves," Hannah told him, but so far, she hadn't done it.

Hannah went to get her purse from the bedroom.

"Now make sure the water's nice and hot when you wash those jars," she called over her shoulder.

"I just remembered something I promised I'd do for Mr. Gilpin," I hollered. "I'll wash those jars as soon as I get back."

"Blue!" Hannah called, but I was already out the door. I'd had an idea.

I jumped on Dolly's back and headed off in the direction of town, but as soon as I was out of sight of the house, I doubled back to the barn, got a pail of grain, and rode to the pasture where I'd just let the cows out.

My spying expedition on the Wright brothers would have to wait at least another day. I had a cow to save.

Daisy let me loop a rope around her horns, but I had a devil of a time getting her separated from the other cows. Whenever I'd rattle the pail to get her attention, all the cows trotted up, bumping me and the pail to get at the grain. I finally managed it by dumping out some of the grain on the ground, and while the cows jostled for it, I dangled the pail in front of Daisy's nose and led her out the gate, shutting it quickly behind me. Once Daisy realized there was a fence between her and the other cows, she lifted her head and bawled. The cows crowded along the gate, bawling back. I rattled the pail again, and Daisy followed me, but she kept looking back over her shoulder.

I held on to the rope as I got on Dolly and dug my heels in her sides, figuring Daisy would follow along behind. But Daisy had other ideas. She dug in *her* heels, leaned back against the rope, and pulled me clean off.

I jumped up, dusting myself off.

"Durn you, Daisy," I yelled. "I'm just trying to save your life, is all."

I remounted, and this time I rattled the pail. Daisy took

a few steps, then leaned back, fighting the rope. I rattled the pail again, and she stepped forward.

I figured I'd be a year older by the time we made it across the pasture: one step, rattle, two steps, rattle. I wondered if that was where the word *cowpoke* came from, because Daisy was even pokier than Dolly.

Being a trapeze artist was suddenly looking a lot better than being a cowboy.

It took forever for us to make our way through the woods and up to the highlands above the lake, where Hannah's great-grandparents had first settled when they came from Scotland. The buildings were gone, but you could still find the old cellar hole and some old fence where Hannah grazed the sheep sometimes to keep the weeds and brush from taking over.

It was my favorite place.

It also seemed like a good place to hide a cow. I didn't think ahead to what I'd do once cold weather settled in— I'd figure that out when the time came.

I got Daisy inside the fence by dumping the grain on the ground. I pulled her up some clumps of clover, too. I knew at some point she was going to start bawling for the others, but I hoped she was too far away from the barn for them to hear her. I also hoped she wouldn't look for holes in the fence.

I wished Nadine were with me, both for the company

and for sharing my plan to save Daisy. (Hannah had a saying, "If wishes were horses, beggars would ride," whatever that meant, but I guessed it had something to do with not wasting your time wishing for things that can't be.) I wasn't sure I could trust Nadine, either, after what she'd done to Raleigh at the rehearsal.

There were apple trees near the cellar hole. I picked some green apples for Daisy and Dolly and tucked a few in my pocket.

I left Dolly cropping grass and found a flat, mossy rock to sit and eat my green apples. I was plumb tuckered out, and it felt good to sit and let the wind cool me down. Even on hot days, there always seemed to be a breeze up here. 'Course that wasn't so nice in the winter, when the wind came straight from the North Pole, and drifts piled up twenty feet high, but it was worth it, living in a place where you felt you were on top of the world.

I braced my hands behind me and leaned back to feel the wind on my face. Under my fingers, I felt the moss and lichen, small bits of gravel, and little grooves in the rock. Maybe those grooves were glacial scratches. Miss Paisley had told us how rock-studded glaciers had scraped over all the mountaintops in Vermont, shaping them, and leaving scratches in the rocks.

I thought Miss Paisley would be impressed to learn that I'd found some glacial scratches. I picked at a couple of pieces of lichen, and a *V* appeared.

I was pretty sure glaciers couldn't spell, so I peeled away a little more of the lichen.

The *V* wasn't a letter: it formed the bottom of a heart instead, and inside the heart, someone had carved M + R.

Who were they, I wondered, and how long had it been since they'd carved their initials? Fifty years? One hundred? Two hundred?

I could almost picture them, a young man and woman, early settlers, sitting here holding hands, dreaming of their future together. Likely *M* and *R* stood for old-fashioned names, probably something out of the Bible, like Moses and Ruth, or Micah and Rachel, or maybe even Methuselah and Rebekah.

I chuckled. Poor little Methuselah. Imagine having to learn how to spell that!

I looked west, at the layers on layers of mountains, like folds in a quilt: Owl's Head in Canada, the spine of the Green Mountains, Jay Peak, Mount Mansfield, Camels Hump, and beyond that to the Adirondacks. A lot of settlers had moved on, heading west. I wondered if M and R had moved on, too, or if they'd stayed right here and lived out their lives.

Someday, I'd fly over those mountains and see what was beyond, too, but right then, sitting on that rock, it was so pretty and peaceful I could see why Hannah's great-grandparents had settled here. Maybe M and R were even Hannah's ancestors. I'd have to ask if she had an M and R in her ancestry. I pictured them cutting hay with scythes, reading and sewing by lamplight, sturdy people, dressed in old-time clothes. Sometimes, when Hannah was pegging out laundry, her dress flapping around her, she looked like the old photographs of her great-grandparents, or' of pioneers that Miss Paisley had shown us.

Hannah would have made a good pioneer, I decided.

Hannah! I suddenly remembered. She was waiting for me to help her with those canning jars!

I pushed Dolly for home, trying to get her to speed up, but Dolly was pretty much a one-speed horse. I spent the time fretting, wondering what I was going to tell Hannah when she noticed Daisy was gone. I knew from watching Humphrey Bogart movies, and reading the Hardy Boys, that I'd need an alibi. Too bad I'd told Hannah I was going to see Mr. Gilpin. I wouldn't dream of asking him to lie for me, but Nadine would do it. If we were still friends. Maybe I could patch things up between us. Sometimes it seemed like that's all I'd been doing the whole summer, patching up our friendship.

But it was Mrs. Tilton, not Nadine, who ran out to meet me as soon as I pulled into their yard.

"Thank goodness," she said. "Everyone's been looking for you. Hannah's in the hospital."

chapter 20

Other than Mr. Trombley, and Esther when she'd had Rodney, I didn't know anyone who'd gone to the hospital. If you were sick or hurt, you either stayed home and got better or you didn't. If you were sick enough to go to the hospital, that usually meant you were going to die. I'd heard Mrs. Wells say that, and Hannah, too.

"Mr. Gilpin took her to the hospital," Mrs. Tilton said. "He found her at the bottom of the cellar stairs, unconscious. That's all I know, except that there were broken jars all around her."

Broken jars. Jars I was supposed to have carried up.

"You'll stay with us, of course," Mrs. Tilton said. "At least until Hannah gets home."

I wondered how Nadine would feel about that, seeing as how we hadn't talked in weeks, but I was too scared about Hannah to worry about that.

I didn't want to stay home with Mrs. Tilton. I just wanted to go to the hospital to see Hannah, but I couldn't. No one under age twelve was allowed.

"Mr. Gilpin will stop by to tell us how she is," Mrs. Tilton said. "You go wash your face, dear, and I'll fix some lemonade for you."

When I came back from the bathroom, I overheard her talking on the telephone.

"I don't know," she said. "I'm waiting to hear from Mr. Gilpin. No, I don't know if they've made any arrangements for Blue, if Hannah were to, well, you know . . ."

I felt my stomach drop. Die. That's what Mrs. Tilton meant. If Hannah were to die.

I slipped back into the bathroom so Mrs. Tilton wouldn't see me, and sat on the edge of the bathtub, feeling trembly all over.

I'd never thought about what would become of me if something bad happened to Hannah. Hannah was the only family I had. I didn't even know my real mama's name.

I heard a little knock on the door and hurried to wipe my nose on my shirt. I didn't want Mrs. Tilton to know I'd overheard her.

Nadine's worried face poked around the door. She came in the bathroom and sat on the edge of the tub beside me. She nudged me with her shoulder.

"I'm sorry," she said. "About saying you didn't have a

father. Of course you *had* one, you just don't know who he was."

I could have said that it was a good thing she had such a big mouth seeing as how she was always sticking her foot into it, but that didn't feel right, what with Mrs. Tilton being so nice for letting me stay there. Besides, it was a comfort having Nadine sit next to me. I gave her a nudge back, letting her know I'd forgiven her.

"You want to play Monopoly?" Nadine asked.

I shook my head. How could Nadine be thinking of games when Hannah might be dead?

"How about Chinese checkers?" she asked.

"No, I don't feel like it," I said.

"I know," said Nadine. "Let's play Crossing the Iron Curtain."

Crossing the Iron Curtain was a game Nadine and I'd invented. We didn't know what the Iron Curtain was—we'd heard it mentioned in movies—but it sounded mysterious and dangerous. I didn't feel like playing that, either, but since I didn't want Nadine to get mad again, just when we were back being friends, I nodded.

So I played, but all I could think about was Hannah. If only I hadn't gone off with Daisy. If only I'd come back sooner and brought those jars up like I was supposed to. It was my fault that Hannah was in the hospital. She *had* to be all right. She just *had* to.

Maybe God was punishing me for stealing Daisy, though it didn't really feel like stealing. I'd just wanted to save her. Or maybe he was punishing me for wanting to trade places with Nadine. I hadn't really meant it. Didn't God know all that? Didn't he know that I didn't want anything bad to happen to Hannah? I'd do anything if only Hannah was all right.

I kept swallowing, trying not to cry, but then my chest hurt. Could you have a heart attack if you were only ten years old?

Mrs. Tilton hugged me.

"She'll be all right, honey," she told me. "Hannah's the strongest woman I know."

Hannah was the strongest woman I knew, too, but even strong people died. Why hadn't Mr. Gilpin come to tell me anything yet?

Mrs. Tilton took wonderful care of me; it wasn't her fault that she wasn't Hannah. She made eggplant Parmesan for supper. I didn't tell her I wished for Hannah's baked beans and brown bread, or her boiled dinner and johnny-cake, or one of my favorites, rumbledthumps, made with potatoes and cabbage.

I choked down a few mouthfuls and then couldn't eat any more. I was waiting for Mr. Gilpin to come by. What was taking him so long?

It was almost dark before we heard his car pull into the driveway.

"She's got three broken ribs, a broken wrist, and she

needed six stitches on her head," Mr. Gilpin told us. "They'll be keeping her in the hospital for a couple of days."

"The poor thing," Mrs. Tilton said. "She's going to be laid up for a while."

"Well, if I know Hannah," Mr. Gilpin said, "it won't be as long as you'd think."

Mrs. Tilton offered Mr. Gilpin a cup of coffee, but he said he needed to get back to work.

"I'll visit Hannah again tomorrow," he said, and looked at me. "Try not to worry."

Mrs. Tilton tucked Nadine and me into bed, just as she had when we were little, and read us *The Secret Garden*.

"It was my favorite book, as a child," Mrs. Tilton said. I didn't tell Mrs. Tilton that Mary Lennox, the spoiled girl in the story, reminded me of Nadine. I also didn't tell her that I liked *Anne of Green Gables* and Laura Ingalls Wilder better than *The Secret Garden*. *Anne of Green Gables* was one of the reasons I'd so wanted to go to Prince Edward Island, to see the place that Anne talked about, the farm where she lived with Marilla and Matthew. Hannah reminded me of Marilla, gruff on the outside but tender inside. Marilla had taken in Anne, too, when she was an orphan, and given her a home.

It was the thought of Anne being an orphan that made me go all shivery. Mr. Gilpin had said Hannah was going to be all right, but what if he was wrong? If Hannah died, I'd

be an orphan, too, just like Anne Shirley. What would become of me then?

Long after Nadine fell asleep, I lay staring up at the ceiling, thinking about summer nights when Hannah and I'd sat
on the porch and she'd pointed out Cassiopeia, Pegasus,
and Cygnus the Swan. I was glad Mrs. Tilton couldn't hear
me sniffling.

chapter 21

Even though I'd slept over at Nadine's a hundred times, it felt strange the next morning to wake up there and know that Hannah wasn't waiting for me at our house.

Mrs. Tilton fixed eggs Benedict for breakfast. They were good, but I would rather have had Hannah's oatmeal and graham rolls.

I dreaded having to go home to do chores. I thought Nadine would walk up with me and help, but she said she wasn't feeling well. What she meant was that she didn't feel like doing work.

I stepped into the kitchen, my footsteps sounding too loud against the silence. The house seemed so empty without Hannah there. As much as I'd always loved being at Nadine's, I wished Hannah was home in *our* kitchen, fixing us breakfast.

What I noticed most, besides how quiet it was, was the

smell. Or lack of smells. The smell of baking bread, and hot doughnuts, and cinnamon, nutmeg, and ginger had always made our house special, and I missed them almost as much as I missed Hannah.

If Nadine and I were playing "What's your favorite thing?" right now, I'd tell her my favorite smell was our kitchen when Hannah was baking, and my favorite sound would be Hannah humming.

The barn seemed empty, too. The cows stood at the back of the barn, jostling each other and lowing to be milked. I leaned against the doorframe, feeling as alone as a body could get, and let hot tears slide down my cheeks.

What with my sniffling, and the cows bumping against the barn, I didn't hear Mr. Gilpin pull into the yard. I wiped the tears off quick with the back of my hand.

Mr. Gilpin was dropping Raleigh off on his way to the hospital to visit Hannah.

"I've told Raleigh to come by here twice a day to help you with milking and any other chores you might need doing," Mr. Gilpin said. "You're happy to help Blue out, aren't you, Raleigh?"

Raleigh bobbed his head up and down.

"Blue True," he said.

Raleigh followed me into the barn. He picked up a milk pail while I let the cows into the barn and hitched them into their stanchions.

Raleigh stood looking at Daisy's empty stanchion, a puzzled expression on his face. So, after chores, when Raleigh and I were sitting on the back of the wagon eating green apples, I told him the whole story, about Daisy being too old, and that I'd hidden her up on the hill—I knew it was safe to tell Raleigh because it wasn't like he was going to be telling Hannah about it—and that I'd have to figure out something different once winter came. I wasn't sure how much Raleigh understood, but he listened, his head tilted, and it felt good to get it off my chest.

I told him other things too: how I was worried about Hannah, and how it really was my fault that Hannah got hurt in the first place because I was supposed to bring up those canning jars.

I told him I was sorry I'd hit him in the head with that stone, and that I'd told Nadine about him being afraid of water. It felt good to get that off my chest, too.

I wondered whether to tell him I was searching for my real mama. The way Raleigh was listening made me wonder if Raleigh understood more than people thought he did.

"Raleigh, I'm going to tell you something I've never told anyone," I said.

"Baby," Raleigh said. "Baby."

My heart sank. Just when you thought you were getting somewhere with Raleigh, he'd say something completely out of the blue. Who knew what he was talking about?

"Never mind," I said.

Out of the corner of my eye, I saw Cat dash into the barn. Raleigh saw her, too.

"Cat," Raleigh said.

"She showed up here a few weeks ago," I said. "Hannah said probably one of the summer people left her."

"Baby," Raleigh said. Was that what he was talking about now, the cat having kittens?

"Yes, Hannah said the cat had kittens. But I haven't found them yet."

"Baby," Raleigh repeated.

"Yes, baby cats," I said, being as patient as I could. "They're called kittens."

But Raleigh shook his head.

"Baby," he said. For some reason, he seemed stuck on that word, and I didn't know what to do to get him unstuck. Maybe if I distracted him.

"Nadine said she's eaten snails before," I said. "Would you ever eat a snail?"

Raleigh wrinkled his nose and shook his head again. At least we agreed on something.

Walking back to the Tiltons', I realized Raleigh had distracted me, too, from worrying about Hannah.

Nadine said she was "feeling much better" when I got back, and she and Mrs. Tilton did their best to keep my mind off worrying. They took me to town for barrettes for my hair, bought me ice cream, and took me to a movie, but my heart wasn't in any of it. I just wanted to be home, with Hannah.

I was thinking of Hannah as I picked a pail of peas, how she loved eating them fresh out of the pod (I did, too). As Nadine and I shelled the peas, sitting on the porch swing, I wished Hannah was in the kitchen making a batch of new potatoes and peas in milk.

"Let's take the inner tube out on the lake," Nadine said, interrupting my thoughts. "We can eat Popsicles as we float along."

I nodded halfheartedly and popped a pea into my mouth.

"You go get the Popsicles, and I'll get the inner tube. Meet you at the beach." She hopped down the steps.

"I want grape, you know," she hollered over her shoulder.

I nodded to her back and reached for the handle on the screen door.

"No, I haven't told Nadine yet," I heard Mrs. Tilton say.

I yanked my arm back and shrank against the side of the house. What hadn't Mrs. Tilton told Nadine yet?

"I know, Mother. I just want Nadine to enjoy one more golden summer here before everything changes."

I knew I shouldn't be eavesdropping, but wild horses couldn't have dragged me away. What was going to change?

"You know how she adores her father," Mrs. Tilton went on. "She was so upset that he wasn't here for her birthday.

I just don't know how I'm going to tell her about the divorce."

It took a second for that to sink in. Divorce! I didn't even know anyone who was divorced.

"Roger says I can have the house—he's already moved out into an apartment—but we'll have to sell the camp here."

I sagged against the wall. Mr. and Mrs. Tilton were getting a divorce *and* selling the camp? Nadine wouldn't be coming to Vermont anymore.

"I have to go, Mother," Mrs. Tilton said. "I think I heard someone at the door."

I couldn't let her catch me eavesdropping, so I hopped over the porch railing and landed in a rosebush. I bit my lip to keep from yelping. I thrashed my way off the bush, the thorns raking my face and arms, and ran around behind the house, down to the water.

Nadine was sitting on the inner tube on the beach, her arms crossed.

"What took you so long?" she asked.

"Um, I had to go to the bathroom," I answered.

"Where are the Popsicles?" she asked.

"Um, I forgot them," I said.

Nadine looked at me suspiciously.

"What's the matter?" she said.

"Nothing," I mumbled.

"How'd you get so scratched up?" she asked. "You look like you were in a catfight and the cat won."

I pretended to laugh, but it came out more like a croak. Nadine's eyes narrowed.

"You're acting funny," she said. "Is Hannah okay?"

"Are we going to float or not?" I said. "Let's go."

"The water's too cold," Nadine said. "Let's play hopscotch instead."

Nadine drew out hopscotch squares in the sand, and we used pebbles.

I tried to concentrate, but the only thing I could think about was Mr. and Mrs. Tilton getting a divorce, and Nadine won all three games.

"You're not even paying attention," Nadine said.

Of course I'm not paying attention, I wanted to tell her. Your parents are getting a divorce!

But I didn't say that.

I dreaded going back to Nadine's house, too, and having to pretend that everything was normal.

My stomach was a jumble for trying to figure out if I should tell Nadine or not, and I hardly touched supper. I kept sneaking glances at Mrs. Tilton.

"Are you feeling all right, dear?" Mrs. Tilton asked. I just nodded.

That evening, after I milked the cows and carried out Cat's bowl of milk, I squatted and talked to her while she ate.

"I don't know if I should tell her," I said. "It's not right to keep secrets from your best friend."

Cat tipped her head, as if she really was listening to me.

"But what if you know *telling* that secret will hurt the person?" I said.

Cat didn't have an answer for me. At least not one that she was telling.

I sighed. This summer wasn't turning out to be anything like what it was supposed to be.

I scooped a pail of grain from the bin. Maybe riding up to check on Daisy would clear my mind and make me feel better.

But it didn't, because when I rode up to the cellar hole, the gate was open and Daisy was gone.

There was no doubt in my mind as to who had taken her.

The Wright brothers.

chapter 22

I couldn't exactly tell Mr. Gilpin, or the sheriff, or anyone else that I was missing a cow, because I'd been the one to take her in the first place. I'd have to find Daisy and bring her home all on my own. I needed to do it fast, too, because I knew she wouldn't be safe with the Wright brothers. Mr. Wright might have already turned her into hamburger.

But my plans to start tracking down Daisy got a wrench thrown into them because of another rehearsal.

Mr. Gilpin had wanted to cancel Saturday's rehearsal, but Hannah said if he did, she'd get out of her hospital bed to run it her own self, so we all went ahead with it, though I was sure I wouldn't be able to remember a single thing I was supposed to do.

Mr. Gilpin wanted to rehearse the Runaway Pond pageant again, so he assembled all of us just below the dam.

"Blue, you'll go downriver and wait in the mill for

Raleigh to rescue you," Mr. Gilpin said. "We'll start digging. Then the dam will go, Mr. Hazelton will shout, 'Run, Spencer, run!' and Raleigh will start running. That's the signal for the Trombley boys to start pulling the wagon, so it looks like the waves are following Raleigh, and they'll keep going all the way to the mill. Okay?"

We all nodded. Except for Wesley and Dennis.

"What do you want me and Wesley to be doing?" Dennis asked.

Mr. Gilpin hesitated. I could just about see his mind working. He hadn't assigned Wesley and Dennis to this particular pageant, but if he didn't keep them busy, they'd think up something to do on their own.

And being the Wright brothers, it wouldn't be a *good* something.

"You can be two of the diggers," Mr. Gilpin decided, and handed them shovels.

Dennis looked disgusted.

"You ought to blow that dam with dynamite," Dennis said. "My dad's got some we could use. Be a sight easier than digging."

Mr. Gilpin made a funny noise in his throat.

"Blow the dam?" he said. "We don't want to 'blow the dam.'"

"You want the lake to run away, don't ya?" Dennis said.

Mr. Gilpin's face turned a funny shade of purple.

"Good God, no!" he said. "You do realize we're just

putting on a play, don't you? We don't want to actually destroy the town!"

From the look on Dennis's and Wesley's faces, I wasn't sure but what that *was* what they wanted to do.

After the Runaway Pond pageant, we rehearsed the Rogers's Rangers attack. I noticed that instead of real tomahawks, Mr. Gilpin gave Dennis and Wesley ones made out of cardboard. They looked disgusted about that too.

Mr. Gilpin drove me home after the rehearsal and brought Raleigh to help me with chores. I'd thought I might choose to stay at our house after they left, instead of going over to Nadine's, but the house seemed too quiet and empty, and as it got darker, I found I didn't want to stay by myself, so I walked down to the Tiltons'.

After playing Chinese checkers with Nadine, I climbed into bed with her, but I couldn't sleep. I waited until I heard Nadine softly snoring (I had *never* told Nadine she snored; even the old Nadine would have been hopping mad about that) before creeping down the stairs, out the door, and up to my house. I grabbed the little blue quilt off my bed and carried it back to Nadine's, tiptoeing up the stairs.

Climbing back into Nadine's bed, I bunched up the quilt and tucked it under my head. Then, and only then, was I able to get to sleep.

That Sunday, after church, I'd planned to look for Daisy, but I didn't because Hannah came home.

I'd been so excited to have her back, but waiting for Mr. Gilpin to drive her home from the hospital, I couldn't sit still. Hannah had only been gone a few days, but it seemed like months. Would she have changed?

Mr. Gilpin pulled into the yard and helped me get her into the house. Hannah leaned heavily on our arms, her face white with pain. She didn't even look like Hannah. She looked thin, her skin wrinkled and sagging. She certainly didn't look like someone who could carry a bag of grain under each arm.

She looked *old*.

Hannah sank back in her chair and closed her eyes. I tucked an afghan around her, the red and white one she'd knit over the winter.

"If you'd only cleaned off those cellar stairs," Mr. Gilpin said, shaking his head.

Hannah winced.

"You know what hurts the most?" she said.

Mr. Gilpin leaned in close, concern etched on his face. Hannah opened her eyes and looked at him.

"Admitting you were right," she said.

Mr. Gilpin grinned.

Hannah needed help with everything, even feeding and dressing herself, but the worst was giving her a bath. I tried not to look at her as I helped her in and out of the tub, but I could feel the blood rush to my face.

"I'm sorry, Blue," Hannah said, and the way her mouth

was set, I knew it was embarrassing her, too. "I hate feeling so helpless."

I thought of Hannah's grandmother being a nurse in the Civil War. If she could help wounded and dying soldiers, I could help Hannah take a bath.

At least I didn't have to worry about cooking. The quilting ladies dropped off casseroles and baked goods every day.

Mrs. Potter came by bringing us supper. I peeked under the dishcloth. Mmmm, scalloped potatoes, and apple brown Betty for dessert. I would have just served up crackers and milk.

"You know, Hannah, I could stay here for a while if you need me," Mrs. Potter said.

I stole a glance at Hannah, hoping Hannah would say yes. It would be such a relief to have Mrs. Potter help Hannah with bathing and dressing.

"Thank you anyway," Hannah said, "but you've got your own family to tend. Blue's taking good care of me."

I straightened my shoulders. I *would* take good care of Hannah, and I wouldn't complain.

"Well, I can see that," Mrs. Potter said, patting me on the head. "But it's a lot to ask a ten-year-old."

"Blue's very mature for her years," Hannah said, and I squirmed. I wondered if she'd feel the same once she found out about Daisy. Well, I was going to try to get it all sorted out so she wouldn't *have* to find out.

But I didn't have time to search. I couldn't leave Hannah—what if she needed help getting to the bathroom while I was gone, or fell? I thought how Hannah had always made running a farm seem so easy. Well, maybe *easy* wasn't the right word; there was nothing easy about farming. Nadine would have known the right word. Hannah had just made the farm run like clockwork. Now it was more like a broken clock.

I don't know what I would have done without Raleigh. Besides all the milking, he helped me hitch up Dolly, and we took turns mowing the two largest fields. I watched the sky with an anxious eye, hoping the hay would dry and we'd be able to get it into the barn before the next rainstorm.

Raleigh repaired broken tools and equipment, oiled Dolly's harness, even weeded Hannah's flower garden, which had gotten overgrown. No matter what, he was always cheerful, and he pitched in on any chore without complaint. He was easy to be around. As long as I didn't ask him to go swimming. Raleigh didn't even like *wading* in the water. He didn't like it when I swam, either. I reminded myself to ask Mr. Gilpin, sometime, to tell me the story of how Raleigh almost drowned when he was a boy. I was glad I wasn't afraid of the water—I couldn't imagine not being able to swim after a long, hot day.

We finished up the last two milkers, and Raleigh helped

me carry the pails to the milk house. While we were washing up, Raleigh looked out the window.

"Cat," he said.

Sure enough, Cat was sitting on top of the hay wagon.

My stomach dropped. When was the last time I'd fed her? Two days ago? Three? How could I have forgotten her?

"Oh, Cat, I'm so sorry!" I said, and hurried to fill a bowl of milk for her, but when I carried it out to her, I saw there was already a bowl on the ground, one of Hannah's good china bowls. I hadn't put it there.

"Raleigh, did you feed the cat?" I asked.

Raleigh nodded.

"Thanks," I said. "I forgot to. I'm glad you remembered."

Raleigh gave me a shy smile, and I wished Mr. Wright could see him right then, see how Raleigh had come by, every day, pitching in to help out with whatever needed doing. I sure didn't see Mr. Wright offering to help us out any. But I wouldn't have wanted Mr. Wright to come by. I didn't ever want Raleigh to hear what Mr. Wright had said about him. Putting Raleigh into a "home" would be the worst thing they could do. Raleigh was happiest when he was outside, working in the garden or haying or helping out at the ball field.

Raleigh pointed to Cat.

"Cat," he said. "Pat cat."

"No, she doesn't like to be patted," I said. "She's wild."

Raleigh shook his head. He patted his chest and motioned with his hands as if patting a cat.

"Pat cat," he repeated. "Pat cat."

I felt a sinking feeling as it dawned on me what he was trying to say.

"You mean *you* patted the cat?" I asked.

Raleigh nodded, and those nice thoughts I'd just had about him faded away like morning fog. All these weeks of feeding Cat and she'd never let me get near her, but she'd let Raleigh waltz in to pat her? It wasn't fair.

"Well, I guess you'd better be getting home," I said. I felt bad saying that—Hannah would be expecting me to invite Raleigh in and feed him, even if it was just crackers and milk—but I didn't feel like inviting Raleigh in. "It's almost suppertime."

Raleigh's face lit up like a lantern. He reached into his pocket and pulled out a Baby Ruth bar, which made me even madder. Raleigh might not have much money, but he had enough to buy candy bars.

Raleigh held the candy bar out to me. He had bought it with his own money. For me.

I felt small inside. Raleigh had so little in his life, and I was being jealous just because he'd patted a cat!

"Thank you, Raleigh," I said. I could have eaten it right there, the whole thing, but I didn't. If Raleigh could be generous, then so could I. I'd share it with Hannah after supper.

154

I took off my boots and stepped into the kitchen. Hannah was gripping the sink, her face white.

"What are you doing?" I almost yelled.

"Getting supper," she said. "I think I can manage our meals from now on."

As worried as I was, I knew there was no arguing with Hannah. Once she had her mind made up, you might as well try to move a granite boulder with a teaspoon.

By the time the baked potatoes and meat loaf were ready, Hannah was too worn out to eat, but she'd proved she could do it. And the next morning, when Raleigh and I came in from milking, she had a pot of hot oatmeal ready for us.

Dr. Hastings stopped by as she was tidying up and scolded her for doing too much too soon.

"Might be time you thought about retiring," he told her. "Sell the farm, get yourself a little place in town. Take it easy."

Hannah picked up her broom and chased Dr. Hastings out of the house.

"Quack," Hannah said. "What would I do if I retired?"

That's when I knew Hannah was going to be all right.

Hannah decided she was ready to start baking again. If I put all the ingredients out on the counter for her, she was able to mix and stir them with her left hand. Once again, the house smelled of cinnamon and nutmeg.

"We need to get back to our regular deliveries, so we

can be adding to your college fund," Hannah fretted, and I felt guilty she'd been worrying about that. Of all my worries—Hannah, Daisy, Mr. and Mrs. Tilton getting a divorce—the one thing I had *not* been worrying about was the college fund jar!

I needed to get the hay in, too. Those two fields weighed heavy on my mind. Even with Raleigh's help, it would take days to get all that hay in the barn. We'd cut too much at one time.

I tossed all night, worrying how Raleigh and I were going to get the haying done by ourselves, and yawned so hard at breakfast I thought my jaw was going to break.

I needn't have worried.

chapter 23

I hadn't even finished my oatmeal when we heard a tractor. Mr. Thompson, Mr. Wheaton, and Esther's husband were the only farmers in the area who had tractors.

Hannah stepped out onto the porch, and I followed behind her, half a graham roll in my hand.

Mr. Green drove his tractor into the yard. I saw three pickups and two cars pull in behind him. Mr. Hazelton, Mr. Gilpin, even Mr. Trombley.

"I might not be much help, but I'll do what I can," Mr. Trombley said. "After all you've done for us."

"He's got one arm, and I've got one leg," Mr. Gilpin said. "Working together, we might just about be worth one person."

"I don't know how I'll stand it," Hannah said. "Sitting here while other folks are doing my work for me."

"Think of it this way, Hannah," Mr. Gilpin said. "You've

always done for others when they needed help. Let them return the favor."

The men headed for the fields, and the women came inside.

"We miss you at the meetings, Blue," Mrs. Fitch said.

"Yes, I hope you'll be coming back," Mrs. Potter said. "We've only got three weeks to get the anniversary quilt done."

"And I'm no help at all with this broken wrist," Hannah said. "But I'm pleased you're here."

I left the women quilting and joined the men in the fields.

Mr. Green hitched up the side-delivery rake and got busy raking while the other men pitched the hay onto the wagons.

Mr. Gilpin and I worked alongside each other with the bull rakes, raking up the stray scatterings of hay.

Huge, billowy summer clouds floated across a sky the color of the bachelor's buttons in Hannah's flower garden, swept along by a wonderful breeze that kept us cool. It would have been a perfect day if only Hannah were out working with us.

I knew the quilting ladies would be watching out for her, but even so, I kept glancing back at the house.

"I know, I worry about her, too," Mr. Gilpin said. "But Dr. Hastings said she'll be fine. Did you hear him tell Hannah she might want to retire?"

I nodded.

"She chased him out with a broom," I told him.

Mr. Gilpin laughed.

"Doesn't surprise me in the least," Mr. Gilpin said. "He's lucky she didn't go after him with one of these pitchforks." And as worried as I was, I had to laugh at the thought of Dr. Hastings running down the road with Hannah waving a pitchfork at him.

"Good to see you laughing," Mr. Gilpin said. "I know you've been awfully worried about Hannah, but I wouldn't be surprised if she outlives us all. She's a remarkable woman."

"Maybe someday you'll write a book about her," I said.

Mr. Gilpin raised his eyebrows.

"Maybe *you* will," he said.

Me, write a book? I was sure the very thought would make Miss Paisley faint dead away.

Birds startled up out of the grass edging the field: red-winged blackbirds, meadowlarks, and Hannah's favorite, bobolinks. She said they sounded like summer. To me, they sounded like someone plucking rubber bands.

"Bobolinks were always my mother's favorite sound," Mr. Gilpin said.

"What's your favorite sound?" I asked.

"Spring peepers," Mr. Gilpin said.

It surprised me to find out my favorite sound was Mr. Gilpin's, too.

"Hannah's is bagpipes," I said. "Her grandpa played them."

"Well, now, I like the sound of the pipes, too," Mr. Gilpin said. "I'd like to learn how to play them."

I looked at him.

"Me too," I said.

"I know a piper we could take lessons from," Mr. Gilpin said. "We'd make quite a sight, wouldn't we, dressed in kilts and leading the parades!"

Oh, wouldn't that make Nadine jealous, me playing bagpipes in a parade!

It was hard to believe I'd been scared of Mr. Gilpin at first. Now he seemed avuncular.

"How'd you lose your leg?" I blurted out, and stood there, my face burning. Had I really just asked him that, I wondered.

"A childhood accident," he said. "I had a tough time accepting it at first. Felt sorry for myself. There're a lot of veterans came home from the war without legs or arms that felt that way, too. But not having a leg doesn't mean you can't have a good life."

I felt ashamed for feeling sorry for myself. At least I had both arms and legs! And Hannah and I had a good life, even if I didn't have all the things that Nadine had.

"Many hands make light work," Hannah said sometimes, and it was true. The haying that would have taken Raleigh and me days to do was done by chore time.

chapter 24

Raleigh stayed after all the other men had left and helped me with the milking. We carried the pails into the house, where we found Hannah listening to some opera singer.

Raleigh put his hands over his ears.

"You don't like that music?" Hannah asked. Raleigh shook his head.

I put on a Glenn Miller record, and Raleigh's face broke into a grin. He started tapping his foot, then he stood and waltzed around the room. Watching him dance, you would have thought he was just like anyone else.

"You're a fine dancer," Hannah told him. "I think you should teach Blue how to dance."

Me? I shook my head, but Hannah nodded at me and motioned me out on the floor.

Raleigh grabbed my hands and started moving his feet, but I stood still, not knowing what to do.

"Just stand on his feet," Hannah said, "until you get the hang of it."

I was nervous at first, and felt about as graceful as a cow, but by the end of the record, I almost knew what I was doing. Raleigh wanted another tune, so I put on a Jimmy Dorsey record, and we glided across the floor, me riding on Raleigh's feet. It wasn't exactly the same as I'd imagined after watching Nadine dancing with Mr. Tilton, but it was something very much like it.

Hannah smiled and tapped her foot, too.

The rest of that week, after Raleigh and I finished chores in the evening, I'd put on a record, and we'd dance until I didn't have to stand on his feet anymore.

"A few more weeks of that, and you'll have the hang of it," Hannah said. "I might even be able to dance *with* you."

I smiled, happy at the thought of Hannah feeling well enough to dance, but the smile froze on my face at Hannah's next words.

"When were you going to tell me about Daisy?" she asked.

Uh-oh. I hadn't even thought up a story to tell Hannah to explain about Daisy. Since Raleigh and I'd still been doing all the milking, I didn't think she would even notice Daisy was missing. I should have known better. Not much got by Hannah.

"I know you're just trying to help me," Hannah said. "But you should have told me. You shouldn't have had to worry about that all on your own. It's the Wright brothers, no doubt, though if they were smarter, they would have known better than to take a *dry* cow."

Hannah thought the *Wright brothers* had taken Daisy! Well, I did, too, but she didn't suspect that *I'd* taken Daisy *first*. I wanted to keep it that way.

"I'll talk to Wallace about it," Hannah said.

"No!" I almost shouted, and Hannah stared at me in surprise. It wouldn't do to make her suspicious, so I reined in my racing heart. "I mean, no, I don't want you having to worry about it, either. I'll tell him when I go into town next."

I had no intention of telling Mr. Gilpin anything about Daisy, but with Hannah feeling so much better and able to do things for herself, this would be the perfect time to work on solving the mystery of the missing animals. Maybe Nadine would like to do some investigative reporting with me. Maybe she'd like to go spy on the Wright brothers with me to see if they had Daisy. And any other animals they weren't supposed to have.

Nadine's face lit up when I asked her. Nadine might talk about her friends back home, but when Nadine was here in the summer, *I* was the only friend *she* had around, too.

"I saw Mr. Wright in town this morning," Nadine said. "He was in the grocery, and Mr. Clark was telling him that they were all out of whatever it was that Mr. Wright wanted, so Mr. Wright stomped out, saying he and his boys shouldn't have to waste an evening going to Hardwick for the feed.

Or maybe he said seeds. Anyway, I don't think they'll be home."

If I'd been thinking straight, I would have seen the holes in this story (like why would Mr. Wright be in the *grocery* asking for feed or seeds) and wondered if Nadine had heard right, but I let my eagerness get the better of me. Nadine and I agreed to meet up at seven o'clock.

I had too many butterflies in my stomach to eat supper. Spying on the Wright brothers had seemed like such a good idea when I first thought of it, but now that we were actually going to do it, I wondered if maybe it was a bad idea. If they found us out, what would they do to us? We hadn't told anyone where we were going. Nadine and I could disappear and no one would ever know.

It felt like an even worse idea when Nadine showed up in a bright yellow rain slicker and white boots.

Why don't you just attach a big spotlight on your head and a sign around your neck that says YOO-HOO, DENNIS AND WESLEY, WE'RE SPYING ON YOU! I wanted to say, but I didn't. I didn't want to ruin the good feeling between us. It seemed like old times, like when we'd played crossing the Iron Curtain, except this time we weren't playing; this was spying for real.

Any other evening, it would have been a beautiful ride, the sunlight painting the tops of the hills a warm gold and casting long shadows across the fields, but I was too nervous to appreciate it. I wished I could come up with a good excuse to turn around and go home, but I didn't want Nadine thinking I was a chicken.

Nadine clung to my arm.

"I hope I don't get any bats in my hair," she said. I didn't say anything, but I thought that bats should be the *least* of her worries.

When the Wright farm came into view, I slid off Dolly and tied her to a bush, then ducked down into a ditch, dragging Nadine behind me.

"Oh, you just got my new boots all dirty," Nadine said.

"Shh," I said. "Besides, they're *rubber* boots."

"Why are we hiding?" Nadine wanted to know. "They're not home."

"I want to make sure before we go walking in there," I said.

Nadine rolled her eyes.

I lifted my head enough so I could scan the yard, the barn, the house, for any sign of movement, but the only thing moving was Nadine, who was acting like she had ants in her pants.

"Quit wiggling," I told her.

"I've got to go," Nadine whispered back.

"You can't go," I told her. "We just got here."

"No," said Nadine, wiggling more. "I mean I have to *go*."

"Oh," I said. "Well, go, then."

"Out *here*?" Nadine said, incredulous.

"Yes, out here," I said.

"I can't go out *here*," Nadine said, shuddering. "There're snakes and spiders and things."

"Oh, for goodness' sake," I told her. "Well, there's the Wrights' outhouse over there. I guess you could use that." I thought it best not to tell her that I thought there'd be even more snakes and spiders *inside* the outhouse than outside.

From the look on Nadine's face, I could tell she was thinking the same thing, but desperate times call for desperate measures. She ran across the yard and opened the door. I decided it was best not to tell her about the hornets' nest hanging under the eaves, right over the door.

Nadine's face scrunched up, and it seemed I could almost smell the outhouse from where I was. Nadine hesitated, then held her breath and popped inside, the outhouse door slapping shut behind her.

Out of the corner of my eye, I saw Dennis come around the corner of the barn. A second later, Wesley followed him.

My heart plummeted to the ground, bounced, and came back up, threatening to bring supper with it. The Wright brothers weren't in Hardwick; they were walking toward the outhouse!

"I tell you, I heard something," Dennis said. "Sounded like the outhouse door."

"Maybe it's another skunk," Wesley said. "Let's put this one in Old Lady Paisley's car."

They were only a few feet away from the outhouse. What was I going to do? I couldn't let them find Nadine in there.

I remembered how Raleigh had rescued that heron from the Wright brothers and how my attempt to rescue *him* had backfired.

I hoped my aim would be better this time. I'd be getting revenge for Dolly, too.

Straight as an arrow, the rock left my hand and ripped into the hornets' nest with a satisfying thunk. Both brothers only had time to glance upward at the sound, and the next second, they were hollering and slapping as angry hornets poured from the damaged nest. Dennis and Wesley took off running toward the house, a black cloud of hornets following them.

Nadine tore out of the outhouse, screaming for all she was worth, but her raincoat and rubber boots protected her from getting stung.

I was having a hard time holding Dolly, what with the hornets and Nadine screaming, but as soon as I'd helped Nadine scramble aboard, Dolly took off toward home faster than I'd ever seen her go. We made it to Nadine's house in record time.

We dashed up the stairs and into her bedroom, slamming the door behind us. We flopped on the floor, panting as if we'd run five miles. That had been way more dangerous than playing crossing the Iron Curtain. I felt like we'd just escaped across enemy lines! We looked at each other and laughed.

Nadine picked up her pillow and threw it at me.

"I can't believe you hit that bees' nest," Nadine said. "Those boys were screaming like little girls." That from a girl who *did* scream like a girl.

I tossed the pillow back at her.

"They were hornets," I said, "and I wouldn't have had to hit it if you hadn't just *had* to go in that outhouse."

Nadine giggled, but then her face got serious.

"I never should have told them about Raleigh being afraid of water," she said. "I'm sorry."

I knew how hard it was for Nadine to apologize, and I smiled at her. I wished we hadn't wasted so much time this summer being mad at each other.

Nadine propped herself up on her elbows.

"With everything going on, it must be hard to concentrate on your column," she said.

I sat bolt upright. My column!

"I forgot all about it," I said.

"I thought maybe you had," Nadine said, "so I wrote it for you."

"Really?" I said. "You did that for me?"

"Sure," Nadine said. "I'd be happy to keep doing it, too, you know, till Hannah's better."

I felt guilty, Nadine having to do my work for me, and I

didn't know what Mr. Gilpin would say about her writing my column, but it sure would take a weight off my shoulders.

"I'll ask Mr. Gilpin tomorrow to see if that's all right with him," I said.

"I'll go with you," Nadine said.

I felt like hugging her. She was a true-blue friend. Which made me feel even worse about keeping secrets from her.

I spotted my blue print quilt on the floor. With everything going on lately, I'd forgotten to take it back home. I bent over to get it, but Nadine was quicker, and snatched it up before I could. She held it at arm's length, wrinkling her nose.

"I can't believe you haven't thrown this ratty old thing away," she said. "Maybe I just ought to burn it."

"No! Give it back," I said, grabbing for it, but Nadine tucked it behind her.

"Not till you tell me why you're saving it," she said.

Maybe it was because I was tired of keeping it a secret, or maybe it was because spying on the Wright brothers had brought us closer, or maybe it was because I wanted Nadine to be the kind of friend that I *could* unburden myself to, but whatever the reason, I told her the truth about looking for my real mama, and about finding out the quilt was the one that I'd been wrapped in, and about Esther and Peddler Jenny, everything, except for the part about her parents getting a divorce.

Nadine listened all the way through without interrupting once.

"So this quilt's a clue," Nadine said. "We can use it to find out who your real mama was."

She'd said *we*. It's amazing how that little word made me feel so much better. I wasn't doing this alone anymore.

Nadine frowned and held the quilt close to her face, squinting.

"What are these letters for?" she said.

"What letters?" I asked.

"Here," Nadine said, "in the corner."

I snatched the quilt out of her hands and held it up to the window so I could see better.

In the corner, three letters stitched in white thread, so tiny it was almost as if whoever had sewn them there hadn't wanted anyone to find them: *MRS.*

chapter 25

"Mrs. who?" Nadine asked, but I didn't know.

All this time, ten years, those letters had been in the corner of the quilt, like a secret.

I wasn't too happy that it was Nadine instead of me who'd found those letters. I'd overlooked a big clue. Didn't make me much of an investigative reporter, did it?

I'd let myself get sidetracked, searching for those missing animals instead of for my mama. Well, that was all going to change, but good.

Why hadn't my mama put her last name on the quilt, too? Had she been in such a hurry that she'd only had time to sew *Mrs.*? Right now, it didn't seem like much of a clue, but it did mean that whoever had left me was married.

Peddler Jenny had been married. But I didn't know her last name, and I was beginning to realize how hard it is to track down someone if you don't know their last name, but at least I had Nadine helping me out now.

If I hadn't known about Mr. and Mrs. Tilton getting a divorce, the evening would have been perfect. Nadine and I built a bonfire on the shore, and we roasted hot dogs on sticks, and then marshmallows to make s'mores, and watched as a few shooting stars zipped across the sky. It was just like old times, and I hated going home, afraid to break the spell.

After chores the next morning, I met up with Nadine, and we rode Dolly into town to talk to Mr. Gilpin. Nadine wasn't her usual talkative self, but I chalked it up to all the excitement of yesterday.

"After we ask Mr. Gilpin about you writing the column for me," I said to her over my shoulder, "maybe we could look through old copies of the paper for more information."

Nadine didn't answer right off, and when she did, it was with a question.

"If you do find out who your mama is, what are you going to do?" she asked.

"Go meet her, I guess," I said. "I want to know why she left me in Hannah's kettle."

Nadine frowned.

"But you aren't thinking of leaving Hannah, are you?" she said. "That just wouldn't be right."

I should have known all that good feeling between us

last night couldn't last. Who was she, with her perfect family, to be telling me what was right or not?

"You see, I was thinking more about your mama last night, after you left," Nadine went on. "I'm not sure you should be looking for her."

What?

"It would be wrong to leave Hannah," Nadine said. "Besides, your mama hasn't come back for you, has she?"

Her words stung me. I thought friends were supposed to support you no matter what. I wished I hadn't told Nadine after all.

"Don't you think that if she was coming back, she would have done it by now?" Nadine said.

That took my breath away. I managed to nod.

"Good," Nadine said. "I'm glad that's settled. Now, let's go talk to Mr. Gilpin about the column."

The rest of the ride into town, Nadine prattled on about the queen's coronation, but I didn't even listen. I kept thinking about what she'd said. Was she right? Was it wrong of me to be looking for my mama?

"How's Hannah doing?" Mr. Gilpin asked, first thing.

"She's sure not taking it easy," I answered. "She was up at four o'clock baking, and I—" I was going to tell him about all the extra deliveries I had to do, but Nadine interrupted.

"Blue has something she wants to ask you," she said.

I thought that was rude of her to interrupt, but I reminded myself that she *was* helping me out with my column.

173

"If it's all right with you, Nadine said she'd write my columns for me," I said. "Just till Hannah's better."

Mr. Gilpin looked at Nadine and then at me.

"Can she write?" he asked me, but Nadine jumped in.

"I write for the school newspaper back home," she said. "Actually, Mr. Gilpin, I'm a much better writer than Blue is."

I glowered at her, but she didn't look my way.

"Well," said Mr. Gilpin. "I don't know about that, but Blue does have a lot on her plate right now. If it's all right with her, I guess it's all right with me. We'll see how you do."

Nadine pulled a piece of paper out of her pocket.

"Actually, I've already got it done," Nadine said. "And I'm partly done with next week's column as well."

Yesterday, having Nadine write my column had seemed like a weight off my shoulders. So why did it feel like a stab in the back today?

When the paper came out on Thursday, people started talking about Nadine's column. Even Mr. Gilpin and Mr. Allard.

I walked into the *Monitor* office just as Mr. Gilpin and Mr. Allard were leaving. They both nodded at me but kept on talking.

"I can't believe she actually used the word *catanadromous*," Mr. Allard said. "I consider myself an educated man, but even I had to look that one up."

"Nothing wrong with educating the public by developing their vocabulary," Mr. Gilpin said.

I went straight to Mr. Gilpin's dictionary, which was already open to the right page. I wondered if Mr. Gilpin had had to look it up, too.

"Cat-a-nad-ro-mous, *adj.* referring to fish that go from salt water to freshwater every year to lay their eggs."

Hmph, I thought. Anybody can look up words in a dictionary. Doesn't make them writers.

Nadine was too busy finishing up next week's column in the evenings to go swimming, or make s'mores, or watch fireflies.

"Well, I'd *like* to, Blue, really I would," she said, "but I've just got too much to do to make this column something people will want to *read.*" Which was an insult no matter how you looked at it.

The second week, Nadine used the words *glossophagine* ("taking food with the tongue, like a frog or an anteater"), *atrabilarious* ("feeling melancholy"), *testudineous* ("slow-moving like a turtle"), *susurrus* ("a whispering sound"), and *ranine* ("pertaining to frogs") all in the same paragraph!

"Nadine's supposed to be writing about people," I told Cat. "Not fish, turtles, and frogs. She's not writing a nature book, for Pete's sake." But I knew if I said anything to Nadine, she'd just get mad.

On my deliveries, I heard other people talking about Nadine's columns, too.

"It's been years since I'd used my dictionary for anything other than a doorstop," Mr. Moulton said.

Riding past the river one day, I saw Mr. Hazelton standing knee-deep in the water, fly-fishing. He grinned and waved.

"Trying to catch me one of those catanadromous fish," he said.

Nobody had talked about *my* columns that way. It looked like Nadine *was* doing a better job than I had.

I could tell Mr. Gilpin was glad to have her there, too, because he told me, "Don't worry about the column. You've got enough to handle right now."

He might as well have said, Don't bother coming back to work.

It had taken about two minutes for Nadine to step in and replace me. Even with knowing her folks were getting a divorce, I was finding it hard to feel sorry for Nadine.

I fussed about it with Cat.

"Who does she think she is?" I asked her.

Cat twitched her tail.

"Maybe she *is* a good writer," I said. "But she didn't have to steal my column."

I made up my mind right then and there that I *was* going to keep looking for my mama, but I wasn't going to talk anymore with Nadine about it. I'd let her think I'd given up on the idea. I was determined to get to Barre, too, one way or the other.

chapter 26

Saturday morning, the sun broke through the clouds just in time for the Old Home Day parade.

All week long, I'd been trying to figure out how to get to Barre. I even considered hitchhiking and jumping on a train like a hobo, but it was Hannah who gave me the answer.

Nadine and I were going to ride in the parade together. She'd decorated her bike with crepe paper streamers. I'd taken strips of red wool, the kind that Hannah used to make rugs, and braided them into Dolly's mane. I'd decided not to say anything to Nadine about her stealing my column, or about solving the missing animals case. I just wanted us to have fun today. I was especially looking forward to the taffy pull and the three-legged race.

Hannah didn't feel up to going to the parade, but she was sending bread and cookies for the bake sale. She handed me a jar of chicken soup.

"And I need you to deliver this to Mrs. Gray. Her mother's very sick, and I thought this soup might taste good to her."

I groaned.

"Mrs. Gray?" I said. "But that's in the other direction."

"Well, it won't take that long," Hannah said.

"But I'll be late for the parade," I said.

"Not if you hurry and stop arguing with me," Hannah said.

I wasn't done arguing by a long shot, but then it hit me. This was the perfect opportunity to ask Mrs. Gray for a ride to Montpelier! From there, I'd find a way to Barre, where I could start looking for Peddler Jenny.

"Okay," I said, and Hannah's eyebrows lifted in surprise.

To get to Mrs. Gray's place, I had to ride two miles out on the other side of town, take a right-hand turn, and go another two miles.

"Oh, that Hannah," Mrs. Gray said, taking the soup. "She's always so thoughtful."

Yeah, I thought, to everybody *else*. Nobody cared if *I* missed the parade.

"Mrs. Gray?" I said. "Are you still going to visit your daughter in Montpelier?"

"No," said Mrs. Gray. "My lumbago's been acting up, so my daughter's going to come visit *me* instead."

My heart sank, and I fumed as I headed back down the

road. Great. I'd wasted the morning on a wild-goose chase. Not only did I *not* have a ride to Barre, but I was going to miss the Old Home Day festivities.

Two miles down, a left-hand turn, and two miles straight back to town, just like one of those right-angle triangles Miss Paisley had shown us in arithmetic. I'd never make it back in time for the parade.

Unless I took a shortcut.

What was that word Miss Paisley had used for the side of the triangle opposite the right angle? It sounded something like *hippopotamus.*

Hypotenuse. Yes, that was it.

I couldn't remember how to figure out the length of the hypotenuse, but it just made sense that it'd be shorter to cut across instead of going back the way I'd come. I rode Dolly past Mrs. Gray's house, across the fields behind the house, and pointed her in the direction I thought town was.

I hadn't figured on there being no road, just dense woods and swamp. Poor Dolly was either knee-deep in mud or scrabbling through thick brush, and goodness knows how many swarms of mosquitoes and horseflies we rode through, and she didn't like it one bit.

She didn't know how to figure out the hypotenuse any more than I did, it looked like.

Just when I thought we were lost for all time, I heard the river, and we came out into a little clearing next to it. In the distance, I could see the church steeple and hear calliope music from the fairgrounds. I wasn't sure whether that hypotenuse had been shorter after all, but I thought Miss Paisley would be pleased to learn I'd used arithmetic over the summer.

I was wondering how we were going to get across the river when we came to a rickety little bridge. It had some boards missing, and to tell you the truth, it didn't look like it'd hold me up, much less a horse. Dolly took one look and said no way was she setting a hoof on that, that she'd wade across the river instead, thank you very much. (Wasn't one of those phobias that Nadine had mentioned a fear of crossing bridges? Well, Dolly had it.) But that bridge got me to thinking. There was a bridge that led to Raleigh's. Was this it? I knew I might be late to the parade, but I couldn't pass up a chance to finally see Raleigh's house. And because I'd be riding Dolly through the swamp, I didn't have to worry about the bloodsuckers.

It was such tough going that I figured Raleigh must have some easier route getting to and from town. Just when I thought I was lost for good again, we came to a house.

It was small and set back in the trees, and from the outside, it looked like it was a bunch of old boards thrown together, a lot like that rickety bridge, but when I looked in the window, everything was neat as a pin. I felt a little disappointed. I'd half hoped Raleigh really did live in a caboose or a tree house.

I walked Dolly down along the river, looking for the best place to cross. I rounded a bend and stopped.

I stared for a long time, not believing what I was seeing.

Under the trees, and spread out along the riverbank, were dozens of pens and cages, each holding a different animal. In one, a heron with a bandaged wing stared at me with beady eyes, and three half-grown heron babies squawked and hopped around her, flapping their wings.

The heron that the Wright brothers had hurt. Raleigh hadn't "dispatched" her, and he'd retrieved her babies from the nest, too.

Some of the bigger pens held pigs and sheep. In one of the smaller cages, a three-legged rabbit munched on some lettuce, and in another cage was a chicken that looked exactly like the hen that Mrs. Wells had given Raleigh. He hadn't turned her into soup after all.

Looking in each pen and cage, I realized that Raleigh hadn't eaten *any* of the animals people had given him. He'd taken care of them and turned them into pets!

I thought of how the Wright brothers had called Raleigh yellow. Well, maybe Raleigh *was* yellow, but at least he had a good heart, which was more than you could say for the Wright brothers.

Around the next bend in the river, I found more animals, but not animals that people had given Raleigh.

Daisy lifted her head and mooed when she saw me.

I ran toward her, laughing. Good old Daisy. The Wright

brothers hadn't turned her into hamburger after all, but how had she gotten away from them? How had she gotten here?

I stopped dead in my tracks.

There was another cow beyond Daisy, a red and white cow with the longest horns I'd ever seen. It took a few seconds before I figured out it was the Texas longhorn Mr. Wright had lost in the swamp and had never been seen again.

Except I was seeing her.

That wasn't all. My eyes moved from animal to animal, like one of those pictures where you have to connect the dots before you can tell what it is.

I guessed that the sheep grazing next to the cows was Mr. Butler's missing sheep, and the calf with a splinted leg was Mr. Lapointe's.

Just past the Texas longhorn was another animal I'd only seen in movies, like *Lawrence of Arabia*. It's not every day you find a camel in a Vermont field, and it took a second for my brain to recognize it, but there it was, a real-life camel, lying down, chewing its cud.

I knew then that if I looked in one of those cages nearer Raleigh's, I'd probably find the monkey, too.

The Wright brothers hadn't stolen the animals.

Raleigh had.

I don't know how much time passed with me just staring at those animals. You would have thought I'd be happy to have solved the mystery, but I wasn't. I couldn't write my article now. If I did, showing that it was Raleigh who'd taken the animals, that just might be all Mr. Wright needed to have Raleigh put away for good.

I left the animals and pushed Dolly as fast as she would go back to town. This was too big for me to figure out: I had to tell Mr. Gilpin. He'd know what to do.

I got there just as the three-legged race finished up. Nadine shot me a look, and I knew I'd hear words later, seeing as how I'd made her miss it. We always seemed to be fighting, but I couldn't worry about that right now. I had to find Mr. Gilpin.

He was busy lining up the veterans for the parade: first, Mr. Emerson, who'd fought in the Spanish-American War; then Mr. Barclay and Mr. Thompson, in their World War I uniforms; and then two rows of World War II veterans. Raleigh stood right in the middle, waving a flag. He had no idea how much trouble he was in.

Mr. Wright was standing off with a group of other men. They had beer bottles in their hands and were talking and laughing, loud.

Looking at him, I could see why Dennis and Wesley had turned out so bad. Made me almost feel sorry for them.

Almost.

Mr. Wright swaggered over and shoved his nose right into Mr. Gilpin's face. I'd seen Dennis do the same thing with Raleigh, so I could see where he'd gotten it from.

"It ain't right, him marching with them," Mr. Wright growled, pointing his bottle at Raleigh. "He ain't a veteran."

I saw the muscles in Mr. Gilpin's jaw moving, but he kept his voice even.

"The *veterans* are fine with having Raleigh march with them," Mr. Gilpin said. "And since you're *not* a veteran, I don't see as you have any say in the matter."

Mr. Wright's eyes got even beadier, and I shivered.

"People like him ought to be locked up," Mr. Wright said. "He's a menace to the law-abiding citizens in town."

I could just imagine what Hannah would say to that.

Menace, my foot. And that man wouldn't know law-abiding if it bit him.

Mr. Gilpin must have been thinking the same thing.

"Menace?" Mr. Gilpin said. "Raleigh wouldn't hurt a fly."

Mr. Gilpin didn't know how right he was. Raleigh probably rescued flies, along with everything else.

"I got some things missing around my place," Mr. Wright said, "and I think he took 'em, things like fence wire, some sap buckets, couple sticks of dynamite. I bet he's been stealing things for years, but no one suspects him because he's everybody's favorite retard."

Mr. Gilpin looked too shocked to say anything right away. No one else said anything, either. Most of what Mr. Wright had said was lies—Raleigh certainly wasn't a menace to anyone, and I didn't think he had taken the buckets or dynamite—but Mr. Wright was right about one thing: Raleigh had been stealing for years. Animals.

I cleared my throat, and both men looked down at me.

"What is it, Blue?" Mr. Gilpin snapped.

I could feel Mr. Wright staring at me with his little pig eyes.

"Nothing," I murmured.

Mr. Gilpin turned his attention back to Mr. Wright.

"If I ever hear you talking about Raleigh again, I'm going to sue you for slander, *and* have you arrested for robbery," Mr. Gilpin said. "We both know who's been stealing things for years in this town, and it isn't Raleigh."

Mr. Wright's face turned bright red. He clenched his fists, and I thought for sure he was going to clobber Mr. Gilpin. But Hannah'd always said if you stand up to a bully, he'll back down, and I guess she was right because after a minute he slunk back to his buddies.

Mr. Gilpin let out a breath. I realized I'd been holding mine, too.

"What a misery he is," Mr. Gilpin said. "Bet his wife died just to get away from him. No, now, I shouldn't have said that; it's just he has a way of getting my dander up. What is it you wanted to tell me, Blue?"

"Nothing," I said again. It wasn't the right time to tell him, with the parade ready to start any minute. I'd tell him later.

"You know, I shouldn't be marching in this parade, either. I'm not a veteran, but I do it to honor Herbert, to make sure he's not forgotten. He was a real hero."

I didn't say anything. I didn't know who he was talking about.

Mr. Gilpin must have seen that in my face.

"Herbert," he repeated. "Herbert Spooner. Hannah's husband."

I didn't know anything about Hannah's husband. There was a picture of him on Hannah's dresser, but Hannah never talked about him. I knew Hannah well enough to know she kept her feelings to herself, but still, you'd have thought she would have said *something* about him.

"A good man, Herbert," Mr. Gilpin went on, "though he wasn't ever the same after he came back. War changes a man, you know."

I didn't remember the start of World War II, of course (I'd just been born), but I did have a few memories of the *end* of the war: horns honking, people hugging and kissing in the street (I'd never seen that before), Hannah crying (I'd never seen that, either), but I didn't remember Herbert coming home.

How could I not remember something like that, I wondered.

"We all thought World War I was going to be the war to end all wars," Mr. Gilpin said. "Then we had World War II, and now here we are, in another war."

Oh. Herbert had been in the *First* World War.

I wondered how the war would change Keith.

Mr. Gilpin kept talking about Herbert, but all I could think about was Raleigh. I'd changed my mind about telling Mr. Gilpin about the animals at Raleigh's. Raleigh *had* taken those animals; he'd broken the law. I wasn't sure that even Mr. Gilpin would be able to keep Raleigh from going to *jail.*

I tried to picture Raleigh in jail. I saw him huddled in a corner, shriveled and dying, like Hannah's begonia that I'd forgotten to water while she was in the hospital. And it would be my fault because I'd squealed on him.

I couldn't take the chance of that happening. I had to keep his secret. To protect him.

". . . pretty soon?" Mr. Gilpin said.

"What?" I asked.

"I must say, you seem distracted today," Mr. Gilpin said. "I said, now that Hannah's doing better, does that mean you'll be coming back to the paper pretty soon?"

I shook my head. Who could think of writing a column with all *this* going on? If only I could put it *in* the paper, I'd have more people talking about *my* column than Nadine even *dreamed* about!

"Nadine's better at writing than I am," I mumbled.

Mr. Gilpin pursed his lips and stared at me.

"Do you know why I've been so hard on you?" he asked. "Because I think you *can* be a good writer."

"But Nadine's better at—" I began, but Mr. Gilpin interrupted me.

"No, she isn't," he said. "She's got a good vocabulary, but she doesn't know how to bring life to the words. Sometimes you can get so focused on the words that you forget the story."

Well, I had a story, all right, except I couldn't write it!

I was worrying so much about Raleigh that I couldn't even enjoy the parade, and the cotton candy tasted like sawdust in my mouth. For once, it wasn't the Wright brothers who'd ruined the day—it was Raleigh. What would happen to him when people found out about all the animals he'd stolen?

Nadine and I rode home together, she on her bike and me on Dolly. Nadine talked the whole time, about parades ("It was a pretty good parade, I guess, for a small town, but you should see the parades I've seen in New York and Washington, D.C.—they took *hours*, they had ever so many giant balloons and floats. I expect they'll be asking me to be the queen on one of those floats . . .") and her bicycle ("It's so old-fashioned. I'm going to have Daddy buy me a new bike, and then you can have this one"), and then she got onto the subject of the Wright brothers.

"You know," she said, "we never actually found any evidence last time. I think we should go on another spying expedition over there. I've got it all planned." But I was only half listening. I kept going back and forth in my mind on whether I should tell her about finding the animals. Best friends shouldn't be keeping secrets from each other, and I was keeping one big secret from her already. But she couldn't tell anyone else, and that's the part that worried me. Nadine was kind of a bigmouth when it came to secrets.

By the time we got to Nadine's yard, I'd decided to tell her. Maybe it'd be easier if I told her *this* one; that way I wouldn't feel so guilty about *not* telling her about her parents' divorce.

Nadine leaned her bike up against the porch. She ran in and got us two Popsicles, and we sat on the steps licking them. I decided to start with taking back my column, then I'd tell her about the animals.

"Thanks for writing my column for me," I said, "but I can write it now."

"That's okay, I don't mind," Nadine said.

"I know, but I told Mr. Gilpin I'd start writing it again," I said.

"Mr. Gilpin said I could do it as long as you needed me to," Nadine said.

"I don't need you to anymore," I said.

"But I've already got it partly written," Nadine said. "And, no offense, but I think Mr. Gilpin would rather have *me* write the columns."

"Mr. Gilpin said he wanted *me* to write the columns

again," I said. That wasn't exactly what Mr. Gilpin had said, but I didn't think Nadine would want to hear what Mr. Gilpin had said about *her* writing.

"I think you're making that up," Nadine said. "You're just mad because everybody liked my columns better than yours."

"Did not," I said.

"Did too!" Nadine yelled. "And you're mad, too, because I've got a father *and* brother and you don't."

"Oh, yeah?" I yelled back. "Well, at least I don't have parents that are getting a divorce!"

chapter 27

As soon as the words were out of my mouth, I wanted to snatch them back, but it was too late.

Nadine's face went as white as the spot on Chrysanthemum's forehead.

"You're lying," she whispered.

"I heard your mom on the phone," I said.

"When?" she asked.

"When I stayed with you," I said. "When Hannah was in the hospital."

Nadine's mouth formed an O.

"That was *weeks* ago," she said. "All this time, you knew and you didn't tell me? You're supposed to be my *friend*." She threw the rest of her Popsicle on the ground, jumped up, and ran inside, but at the door, she turned back.

"You know, you were only my best friend here because

no one else was around," Nadine hissed. "Back home, I have lots better friends than you."

I stood, too stunned to say anything, and watched her slam the door behind her. I'd always been afraid that was true, that Nadine was *my* best friend but that I wasn't hers, and she'd just admitted it.

I felt like one of those shell-shocked soldiers I'd seen in old magazines, eyes wide open but empty. I didn't even remember walking home. Once there, I went into the barn instead of the house so Hannah wouldn't see me. I crawled into a corner of the hayloft and cried myself dry.

That night, not even tucking the blue quilt under my head could make me sleep. Tossing and turning, I couldn't help but think that telling Nadine about the divorce had been every bit as mean and thoughtless as she'd been to me.

All the next day, I moped through church and Sunday school and around the house, my feelings going between angry and guilty and back again.

"I know I hurt her," I told Cat. "But she hurt me first. Besides, she doesn't even *want* to be friends with me. Who needs her, anyhow."

Two days passed with no sign of Nadine. My anger had simmered down, and now I mostly just felt sad.

My column was due in one more day, and I hadn't written a single news item for it. Now that I *had* to write my column again, I didn't feel like it. All I could think of was Nadine and how much I'd hurt her.

Last time, our fight had been Nadine's fault—in fact, *most* of the fights had been Nadine's fault—but this time it was mine. Even if we weren't friends anymore, I felt I needed to write her an apology.

I got out a piece of paper, but couldn't think of anything to say, and decided I needed to look in Mr. Gilpin's dictionary for the right words.

Hannah sent me into town with some deliveries, so afterward, I swung by the *Monitor*.

Next to the dictionary on Mr. Gilpin's desk was a photo of an old plane with a young woman sitting in the seat.

"That's Hannah," Mr. Gilpin said. He was looking at the picture so he didn't see my jaw drop. I looked closer, squinting.

"She was a daredevil," Mr. Gilpin said. "In 1911, the first plane came to the fairgrounds, and the pilot offered to give rides. It was awfully gusty that day, and Roy Allard said a person would have to be a fool to go up in that contraption, but Hannah went up.

"After that, Hannah was just crazy for airplanes," Mr. Gilpin went on. "She wanted to learn how to fly. She could have been another Amelia Earhart."

"Why didn't she?" I asked.

"After her father and brother died, Hannah had to help her mother run the farm," Mr. Gilpin said.

So Hannah had had to give up her dreams. Maybe that's why she wanted me to go to college so much.

I wished Nadine and I were still friends so I could talk to her about it. Cat was a good listener, but all my conversations with her were one-sided.

It took me an hour looking through Mr. Gilpin's dictionary to come up with the words I wanted to say. I chewed on the end of my pencil and then wrote:

> *Dear Nadine,*
> *I am contrite, remorseful, regretful,*
> *and penitent, but mostly I'm sorry.*
> *Your friend,*
> *Blue (which is how I feel, too)*

On the way home, I tucked the letter into the Tiltons' mailbox.

All the next day, I waited for Nadine to come over, but she didn't. Maybe they hadn't found my letter yet, I thought, but when I checked their mailbox, the letter wasn't there. I did chores, sneaking glances toward their camp and hoping I'd see Nadine walking up the road, smiling, ready to make up.

"Maybe she just said all that because she was mad," I told Cat. "Maybe she really *didn't* mean I wasn't her best friend, and she's sorry about what *she* said, too."

Cat scratched behind her ear with her hind leg.

Over the next two days, I must have checked our mailbox a least a dozen times.

"What's gotten into you?" Hannah asked. "I declare, you're as jumpy as Cat."

Finally, on the third day, when I'd just about given up hope of Nadine ever answering me, I found a letter on our porch steps. I took it up to my room so I could read it in private.

> *Here are the words that describe you: sneaky, treacherous, traitorous, underhanded, perfidious, unctuous, and mendacious.*
>
> *NOT your friend,*
> *Nadine*

My throat stung the whole time I spent ripping that letter into tiny pieces.

I carried out a bowl of milk to go talk with Cat.

"Nadine must have spent *two* hours looking up all those words," I said. "*Sneaky* and *underhanded* I get. But *per-fid-i-ous* and *men-da-cious*?"

Cat finished her milk and sat down, watching me.

"I told her I was sorry. A *real* friend would have forgiven me. I forgave *her.*"

Cat licked her paw and washed her face.

"I guess you're the only friend I have now," I told her. "Even if you're not a very *friendly* friend."

I made my deliveries and rode home by the ball field, hoping to see a game, but no one was there.

I rode by Nadine's house on my way home, hoping she'd be outside and we might start talking to each other.

I didn't think I could feel any worse, but I was wrong.

A big sign was tacked up on the Tiltons' mailbox.

FOR SALE.

I hadn't thought it would really happen. I guess I'd thought that, somehow, Mr. and Mrs. Tilton would get back together, or that Mrs. Tilton would decide to keep the camp, or that Nadine had her mother and father so wrapped around her finger that she'd find a way to keep the camp, too. But that FOR SALE sign made it real. They were actually going to sell the camp, and never come back.

I lay awake a long time that night, my mind racing with *if-onlys*.

If only I hadn't tried to get my column back from Nadine. Then none of this would have happened. If only Hannah hadn't gotten hurt. Then I wouldn't have had to *have* Nadine write my column in the first place. If only Mr. and Mrs. Tilton weren't getting a divorce. Then I wouldn't have had to keep a secret from Nadine. If only, if only, if only. One word, one little event, can change everything. Two words, FOR SALE, meant I was losing my best friend forever.

I thought of how many times our lives depend on one little event. What if my mama had decided to keep me after all? What if she'd left me in some *other* person's yard? What if Hannah hadn't found me?

I thought of Hannah flying in that airplane in 1911. What if that plane had crashed? Hannah never would have been *around* to find me and take me in.

Mr. Gilpin was right. Someone *should* write a story about Hannah. I should ask her what it was like to fly in that plane, and what it was like to shake Teddy Roosevelt's hand, and if he said anything to her.

The more I thought about Hannah, the more I thought about the other stories the quilting ladies had told about the women in *their* families. If I couldn't write my article about the missing animals, at least I could write those stories. They'd be more interesting than my columns, and they seemed like the kind of stories that other people, from other towns, might want to read, too. Mr. Gilpin hadn't written up those stories for the pageant, but they deserved to be told, just as much as Colonel Barton's, or Alexander Twilight's, or even Spencer Chamberlain's. Esther was right: they were stories that really shouldn't be forgotten.

I slipped out of bed and found my Big Chief tablet and pencil. Sitting back in bed, I wrote down story after story, trying to remember everything the women had said, not using big words, just telling the stories the way the quilting ladies had told them.

I wrote down as much as I knew of Hannah's story, too, her grandmother coming from Scotland, Hannah shaking Teddy Roosevelt's hand, and how she might have been another Amelia Earhart if her father hadn't died.

I'd forgotten most of the dates and wondered if I could find some of them in the old newspapers. And I really had meant to look up those articles that Mr. Webster had written. Maybe they'd give me an idea of how to write my stories better.

It was time I found out about my history, too, and that's when I decided. First thing in the morning, I'd ride to the train station and buy a ticket to Barre. I could use the money I'd earned from writing my column.

The next day, as I rode to town, Dolly tried to go into the Tiltons' yard, but I kicked her with my heels to keep going past.

It was on the way to the train station that I thought of a problem. Mr. Blanchard, the ticket agent, would be sure to ask questions as to why I was traveling to Barre all by myself, and word would get back to Hannah. Maybe I'd better buy my ticket at *another* train station, one where they didn't know me. Except that would take me an extra hour to ride to the next town, so I'd have to wait till tomorrow to do that.

Red, white, and blue banners were already being put up throughout town, and tents were going up at the fairgrounds, getting ready for the sesquicentennial.

Mr. Gilpin looked up from his desk when I walked in, gave a nod, and went back to writing.

Raleigh was sweeping up.

"Baby," he said. Oh, no, he was on that again.

"No, I haven't seen Rodney, and I didn't see any other babies on the way over here," I said, and hurried past him before he could say anything else.

I found the story and pictures of Teddy Roosevelt coming to the fairgrounds, and the pictures of the old plane that Hannah had taken her ride in. I searched again through all the newspapers for 1941 to see if there was anything I'd missed about Peddler Jenny (there wasn't). I wasn't sure what year Mr. Webster had written his articles, and there were too many stacks to search through. Besides, my head hurt from looking at all those old newspapers. I'd have to come back another day.

Standing up, I toppled over a stack of newspapers. They skidded and scattered across the floor like a lava flow. Stupid old newspapers. I kicked at the pile and another stack toppled over. I stamped my foot. It was going to take me at least two hours, I bet, to gather them back up and put them all in order.

I got on my knees to start sorting them and saw a photo with the words DEATH NOTICE over it, but it was the name underneath that caught my eye: Herbert Spooner.

Hannah's husband. I looked at the date on the paper. September 7, 1938. That was three years before Hannah found me.

I sat down on the newspapers and read the whole article, about how Herbert had been wounded in the First

World War; had been awarded the Distinguished Service Cross for extraordinary heroism in action near Saint-Mihiel, France; had worked at the post office for twenty years; was an elder at the Presbyterian church; and would be interred in the East Craftsbury Cemetery. But it was the next sentence that made me stop breathing.

"He leaves a wife, Hannah, and a daughter, Myrtle Rose."

chapter 28

The stairs creaked.

"Blue," Mr. Gilpin said. "I was . . ." But his voice trailed off when he saw the article in my hand.

I ran up the stairs, pushing past him, into the *Monitor* office. Raleigh looked up, startled, from his sweeping.

"Blue," Mr. Gilpin said again, and I spun to face him.

"Why didn't you ever tell me Hannah has a daughter?" I said, and Mr. Gilpin's expression changed to that of a boy who's been caught stealing frosting off a cake.

"Myrtle," Raleigh said, and it was my turn to feel stunned. The only words I'd ever heard Raleigh say were *Blue True*, *baby*, and *pat cat*.

So. Even he knew. If Raleigh knew, everyone in town did. Everyone except me.

I hated Raleigh then. I'd trusted him, I'd even tried to *protect* him, but he'd lied to me, he and Mr. Gilpin and

Hannah and everyone in this town. They'd pretended to care, but all along, they were just a bunch of liars.

"Where is she?" I asked.

"California, I think," Mr. Gilpin said.

"How come I've never heard of her?" I asked. "Why hasn't she ever come back?"

"I think you'd better ask Hannah about that," he said.

"What, so she can just lie about it some more?" I said, and turned toward the door, fighting back tears.

"Wait," Mr. Gilpin said. "Let me explain."

Raleigh stepped in front of me, waving his hands out to get me to stop.

"Blue True," he said, but I pushed past him. He reached to grab my arm, but I snatched it away.

"Don't touch me, you stupid ret—" I caught myself before I'd said it, but Raleigh jerked back like I'd punched him.

"Blue!" Mr. Gilpin thundered.

I ran out the door and leaped on Dolly's back, digging my heels into her sides. She blew out a long breath, surprised, and trotted a few bone-jarring yards before settling back into a slow walk.

"Blue!" Mr. Gilpin called after me, but I didn't stop.

Dolly might have been slow, but my mind was racing. Why hadn't Hannah ever told me she had a daughter?

I rode up to the highlands, found my mossy rock, and sat looking over the valley, but it didn't really help. I'd always loved it up there, but now it seemed like a lie, too.

From up here, at a distance, everything looked so pretty, but all you had to do was look close to find people who were mean and told lies, just like anywhere else.

Sitting there, my fingers tracing the carving of the heart and the two initials, I wondered what had happened to whoever had carved it. Had they lived to be old, or died young, like so many of the people back then? What had their life been like? Had it been full of love and happiness, or had it been weighed down with heartache instead?

When I finally rode home, Hannah was in her flower garden, her arms full of yellow roses and lilies.

"Aren't these just the prettiest things?" she said, smiling.

Myrtle Rose. It made sense that Hannah had used flower names for her daughter. But why had she just named me Blue? Why not Lily or Iris or Violet?

Hannah looked over at me and frowned.

"You all right, Blue?" she said.

I stared at her. All this time, I thought I'd known her. I'd trusted her, completely. I *loved* her. But she'd been lying to me all these years. What *else* hadn't Hannah told me?

There was so much I wanted to ask her. But I didn't. I turned and went to the barn instead.

Cat ducked behind one of the milk cans. I squatted down and waited. Cat poked her head back out. When I didn't move, she sat down, watching me.

She'd kind of betrayed me, too, letting Raleigh pat her, but I didn't have anyone else to talk to, so I told her all the questions I had about Hannah and Herbert and Myrtle Rose. Cat didn't have any answers, but she tipped her head to the side and listened.

I did all my chores, milking, feeding the calves, my mind trying to solve why Hannah's daughter had disappeared and never come back. Had she and Hannah had a fight? Had Myrtle done something bad?

All through supper, Hannah kept looking over at me, but I didn't say anything.

It took a long time for me to fall asleep that night, and when I did, I had dreams of a dark-haired woman sewing letters into the corner of a quilt. *MRS, MRS, M R S.*

My eyes snapped open and I sat upright.

M R S.

Myrtle Rose Spooner.

chapter 29

I don't think I slept a minute the rest of the night, questions piling up in my mind like a snowdrift, but all of them melted away when it came to the biggest question of all.

Was Myrtle my mother?

Maybe there was another explanation. Maybe the person who'd wrapped me in that quilt had exactly the same initials as Myrtle. Or maybe Myrtle had made that quilt for someone else and that person had used it to wrap me in the quilt.

You don't believe that for one minute, the little voice in my head said.

I tugged too hard while milking Iris, and she kicked over the milk bucket. I didn't even care. All I could think about was Myrtle, wondering how I could find out for sure if she was my mother. I'd have to meet her before I could be certain. But how? Where was she? Was she even still alive?

I stared hard at Hannah while she bustled around fixing breakfast.

Did she know? Was she ever planning to tell me about Myrtle Rose?

My very next thought made me feel short of breath.

If it was true that Myrtle was my mother, then Hannah was my real *grandmother*.

Had she ever planned to tell me *that*?

I opened my mouth to ask her, but then I shut it right up again. Hannah had kept this secret for ten years. How could I trust anything she told me now?

"You're looking a little peaked this morning," Hannah said. "You feeling all right?"

No, I wanted to scream, but I just nodded. I didn't think I could speak a word anyway.

"Maybe you need a dose of castor oil," Hannah said.

What I need is someone to tell me the truth, I thought, but I just shook my head.

Hannah had orders for me to deliver, but I went first to the *Monitor* office (I'd been afraid of seeing Raleigh after what I'd said, or almost said, to him, and breathed a sigh of relief that he wasn't there) and marched right up to Mr. Gilpin's desk.

"You knew about Myrtle," I said. "All this time, you knew, everyone in town knew, and no one ever told me."

"Blue—" Mr. Gilpin began, but I didn't let him finish.

"You were all laughing at me behind my back."

"No one was laughing at you, Blue," Mr. Gilpin said, but I didn't believe him. "It was Hannah's place to tell you, not ours."

"Then why didn't she?"

Mr. Gilpin shrugged.

"Every family has secrets," he said.

I delivered the rest of Hannah's orders but hardly noticed where I was, and I could barely speak to Mrs. Wells, Mrs. Thompson, and Mr. Hazelton. I was mad at them, all of them. No one had told me the truth.

Maybe that's how Nadine was feeling, too, because I hadn't told *her* the truth.

Mr. Gilpin's words went round and round in my head.

Every family has secrets.

I'd kept secrets all summer, too, but none of them seemed like anything compared to *this* secret. The other thing I'd found out about secrets was that they have a way of coming out.

Back home, I counted up how much money I'd saved over the summer.

Eight dollars and thirty-three cents. I didn't know how much a train ticket to California cost, but I was sure it was a lot more than eight dollars and thirty-three cents.

Right then, I decided I wasn't going to wait until I earned enough to get me to California. I'd go as far as eight dollars would take me, then sneak onto trains like a hobo. I didn't know how I'd ever find Myrtle, but I was going to try, and I'd find out from her whether she was my mother or not.

The sesquicentennial celebration would be a perfect time to leave. Everyone would be in town, and it would be hours before anyone noticed I was missing. *If* anyone noticed I was missing.

I had to pack in secret, so Hannah wouldn't see. I thought hard about what to take because I knew I had to travel light. I stuffed dungarees, shirts, and a sweater into a grain bag and hid it in my closet. I'd have to leave my books. I figured Myrtle would buy me new books when I got to California.

If she really was my mother.

Maybe it was just because I'd been waiting and watching so many years for my mother, and maybe it was because I wanted so much to believe that Myrtle *was* my mother, but I heard the little voice say:

She is.

And I believed it.

At milking time, I patted the cows and hugged Dolly, already missing them. I planned on riding Dolly to the train station, figuring either she'd walk back home on her own or someone would return her. I'd miss her, but maybe Myrtle would buy me a horse, too.

I didn't think Myrtle would buy me cows.

I thought how things would be here after I left: Raleigh would keep helping around the *Monitor*; Mr. Gilpin would keep trying to scoop Mr. Allard on stories, Mrs. Wells would keep telling her boring stories, the quilting ladies would keep meeting and quilting, the Wright brothers would keep tormenting kids and animals throughout the town. It made me feel hollow inside, realizing my leaving wouldn't change anything. Hannah would be farming by herself again, but everyone would pitch in to help, just like they had when she was in the hospital. She'd get by, and things would go on pretty much as they always had. It would be almost like I never existed at all.

I tried to cheer myself up with thinking of all the new things I'd be seeing, like the sun setting on the Pacific Ocean, and Hollywood stars driving by in their fancy cars. I might even get Humphrey Bogart's autograph!

I tried *not* to think about how much I would miss Hannah.

I didn't want to leave without trying to make things right between me and Nadine, either. It took me a while to work up enough courage to walk over and knock on the Tiltons' door.

Mrs. Tilton answered.

"Is Nadine here?" I asked. "I came to apologize."

Mrs. Tilton looked at me, sadly.

"I'm sorry, Blue," she said, "but Nadine doesn't want to talk to you. I'll tell her that you're sorry, and I'll try to get her to come over to talk to you, but I'm not promising anything."

I nodded and stumbled down the steps. Even if Nadine did come over (and I was pretty sure she wouldn't—she could be awfully stubborn), I'd be gone. I wondered if Nadine would miss me once she realized I was gone for good.

I knew I'd miss her, even with the fights we'd had. Through the summers I'd known her, we'd had more good times than bad.

"Blue?" Mrs. Tilton said, and I turned.

"You're the reason we've kept coming here all these years," Mrs. Tilton said. "Nadine's never been good at making friends—goodness, I don't have to tell you that she's not the easiest person to get along with—but having you for a friend has made all the difference for her. Thank you."

Nadine had bragged about all her friends in Washington, D.C., and New York, but I think, deep down, I'd somehow known that wasn't true, either. She'd needed me for a friend as much as I'd needed her.

I was thinking so hard about Nadine that I didn't see the dark car pulling into the driveway, and jumped sideways at the last minute to avoid getting hit.

I was surprised to see Mr. Tilton behind the wheel. Did his showing up mean the Tiltons *weren't* getting a divorce? Maybe they wouldn't be selling the camp after all. Well, it didn't matter now. I'd be gone, but at least Nadine would be happy about her parents getting back together.

I waved, but Mr. Tilton just stared straight ahead like he

didn't see me, and he didn't wave back. That didn't seem like him. Maybe Nadine had told him what I'd said, and he was mad at me, too.

I stood and watched as Mr. Tilton pulled into the yard. Nadine came flying out of the house screaming "Daddy!" and ran into his arms. He kissed her and put his arm around her shoulders as they walked together into the house.

Tears stung my eyes. I wondered if my reunion with Myrtle would be anything like that.

I stumbled home and slipped upstairs, my heart feeling as heavy as one of Hannah's old sadirons. I'd always thought Nadine and I would be best friends forever; now I didn't have a friend in the world.

I sat at my desk and pulled out my Big Chief tablet. My heart wasn't in it, but I knew I ought to finish writing up the stories of the town mothers before I left. Maybe working on them would help take my mind off Nadine, I thought, but just as I began writing, Hannah called up the stairs for me to help her with the firewood instead.

She split while I piled it in the woodshed. Hannah said firewood warmed you three times: when you cut it, when you split and piled it, and when you burned it. I felt guilty when I thought how Hannah would have to fill up the wood-box by herself this winter—I wouldn't be around to help.

"Storm's coming," Hannah said. "Feels like it'll be a real glysterie."

I did chores as usual, and carried a bowl of food out to

Cat. I wanted to tell her about my plans for finding Myrtle, but Cat wasn't by the barn. I was already late with my deliveries, so I had to leave the food.

Dolly knew the storm was coming and moved along faster than she usually did. I wanted to get home before the storm hit, too. I hoped it would be over before morning. It would be too bad if the sesquicentennial got cancelled. Besides, I didn't want to have to ride to the train station in the rain.

I'd hoped to see Cat waiting by the barn when I got home, but she wasn't. I put Dolly in the barn and scooped some grain into her feedbox. I wondered if Dolly would miss me when I was gone. I knew I'd miss her.

I realized Cat wasn't in the barn, but I looked anyway. Hannah noticed my worried expression when I came in.

"Did you see Cat today?" I asked.

Hannah shook her head.

"She may be off hunting," she said, but I knew something was wrong. Hannah held my supper, warming, while I searched through the orchard and the fields, calling until it got dark. The thunderstorm moved in, the wind whipping the rain sideways (a real glysterie, just like Hannah had said), and I came in, *looking* like a drowned cat and more worried than ever.

After supper, I stood on the porch, the rain drumming on the roof and falling in sheets off the porch.

"Cat! Cat!" I called, my voice echoing in the darkness.

I'd wondered if Cat would miss me, too, but I guessed not since it looked like she'd already left.

"You'll catch your death out here," Hannah said. "Come in and get warm." She turned on the radio and heated some milk on the stove, and we drank cups of hot cocoa while listening to Duke Ellington and Nat King Cole.

I wondered what music Myrtle liked. Would she and I listen to Johnny Ray and Patti Page instead? I pictured Myrtle holding my hands and teaching me how to do the jitterbug and the Lindy Hop.

I looked over at Hannah. She was humming and tapping her foot, and I knew I was going to miss nights like this.

chapter 30

I kept stealing glances at Hannah, trying to make sure I locked her image in my brain so I'd never forget her. I tried not to think how Hannah's heart might break into flinders when I left.

A gust of wind shook the house, and the rain sounded like bullets on the roof.

"I declare, I haven't seen it rain this hard since the '27 flood!" Hannah said. "That's certainly going to put a damper on all the celebrations. And after Mr. Gilpin's worked so hard."

I thought how upset Mr. Gilpin would be if the Runaway Pond pageant were washed out by a real flood!

"You know, after the celebration, I was thinking of starting another quilt," Hannah said. "My wrist has probably healed enough. Maybe you'd like to help me with this one."

I nodded, even though I knew I wouldn't be around to

help with this quilt or any other. The clock chimed nine times.

"Time for bed," Hannah said, as if it were a regular night. As far as she knew, it was.

"Good night," I said, when what I really wanted to say was, Goodbye.

In my room, I tried to write a note to Hannah, but I couldn't find the words, so I crumpled up the paper and threw it away. I hoped she'd know how I felt about her. You can be mad at someone and still love them.

I folded the quilt and put it in my bag of clothes. I also added a photograph of me and Hannah having cotton candy at the county fair. Mr. Gilpin had taken the picture when I was four years old. I'd gotten more cotton candy in my hair than in my mouth.

I heard voices downstairs. One of them sounded like Mrs. Tilton. Had Nadine changed her mind, I wondered.

I folded the stories I'd written and put them in a drawer. Being a writer had been a foolish dream. Once I got to California, I'd go back to my plans to be a lion tamer after all, or a trapeze artist.

I heard Hannah's footsteps on the stairs. I shoved the bag I'd packed under the bed just as Hannah walked in. From the look on her face, I knew that something awful had happened.

"Keith," Hannah said, her voice cracking. "He's MIA, missing in action."

Missing in action. What did that mean, exactly, I wondered. Was Keith dead?

"The telegram was delivered to Mr. Tilton last night, and he drove up to tell Mrs. Tilton and Nadine," Hannah continued. "They'll be driving home tomorrow. Mrs. Tilton just came by to tell me, and to say goodbye."

I closed my eyes, memories of Keith moving through my mind like a movie: how he'd do perfect jackknife dives off the dock; that time he came over wearing his father's fedora to do an impersonation of Humphrey Bogart for Hannah; diving for, and catching, a line drive to the outfield, and then holding it up, triumphant, his laugh like the strike of a match. I couldn't imagine never swimming with him again, never hearing another one of his silly knock-knock jokes, never seeing him again.

It wasn't fair. Keith was so smart and handsome, fun and funny at the same time. It was too bad we couldn't trade him for Raleigh.

The minute I thought it, I was ashamed, but it made sense, really. Why couldn't it have been Raleigh instead? Raleigh wasn't going to get any better, and Keith had so much to look forward to. He would have gotten married, had kids, found *his* calling. Raleigh would never have any of that.

I was sure I wouldn't be able to fall asleep, but I must have because I woke to sunshine streaming through the window and the sky washed clear and clean. The sesqui-centennial would go on as planned.

And I'd be leaving forever.

My arms and legs felt like lead as I dressed. This would be the last time I'd wake up in this room. The last time for a lot of things.

I made myself smile as I went down the stairs, acting like it was just an ordinary day, but my smile felt as painted-on and fake as a clown's.

At breakfast, Hannah looked sad, and I knew she was thinking about Keith. I tried not to think about how she'd look later, once she found out I was gone, too.

I wouldn't be missing in action, just missing.

I wondered if the Tiltons had already left for home. Well, they were all in my past now. I had to start looking at my future, a new future with Myrtle.

"Well, I'll be headed into town now," Hannah said. "I'll see you later on."

"Okay," I said carefully, afraid my voice would give me away.

I watched Hannah drive out of the yard, and the lump in my throat seemed as big as a baseball.

I threw my bag of clothes over my shoulder, feeling a little like a hobo from the Depression, and stood at the door, drinking in the sight and smell of the kitchen for the last time. My eyes fell upon my college fund jar.

Enough money to get me all the way to California and then some.

Don't even think it, the voice of good Blue said.

Take it. It's *your* money, said bad Blue.

It's stealing.

I'll send it back when I get there.

You know you won't.

Think of all the years Hannah worked to earn that money.

She earned it for me.

She saved it for you to go to college.

I'll go to college in California.

It's wrong and you know it.

Shut up.

I tucked the jar under my arm and slipped out the door.

chapter 31

As I rode along, I said goodbye to each place I passed. Goodbye, Mrs. Wells. I'd almost miss her boring stories. Goodbye, Mr. Hazelton. I'd wanted him to give me more lariat lessons; if I was going to be a cowboy, I'd have to get better at lassoing cattle. Well, maybe I'd stop off in Wyoming, on my way to California, and find someone who could teach me.

I passed through town and headed out along the river. The wildflowers were so pretty, lining the riverbank: blue chicory and daisies and black-eyed Susans. California would have other flowers, but they probably wouldn't be as pretty.

Goodbye, river.

I saw the rickety bridge to Raleigh's house up ahead. Goodbye, bridge. Goodbye, Raleigh.

I pictured everyone at the celebration. I imagined the pageants unfolding, seeing in my mind Raleigh running down along the river as Spencer, and wondered who Mr. Gilpin would have fill in for me as Mrs. Willson. I wondered, too, if the Wright brothers would cause some unexpected surprises.

Speaking of which, that's what I was going to be when I found Myrtle. An unexpected surprise. I'd always imagined her face when I finally found her—astonishment turning into joy.

But what if it wasn't? I'd been so busy thinking about our reunion that I'd never let myself really think about what Nadine had said that had made me so mad at the time. What if Myrtle really *didn't* want me back? If Myrtle really *was* going to come back for me, she would have done it by now. And what if, after I got there, Myrtle left me somewhere again? What would I do then?

I thought of all I was leaving behind: Nadine, Mr. Gilpin, the *Monitor*, Raleigh, and especially Hannah. All that for a woman I'd never met. I was leaving Hannah for a woman who'd left me.

I shook those thoughts out of my head. Everything would turn out all right, I told myself. I'd find new people in my life, new kids to play with. Myrtle might even have some other kids.

I pulled Dolly to a stop.

I hadn't thought of that before. What if Myrtle was married and had a family? She probably hadn't told any of them about me. Myrtle might have planned to go to her grave with her secret. If so, she might not be too happy about me showing up and turning her life upside down.

Myrtle hadn't wanted me when I was born. What made me think she'd want me now?

As mad as I was at Hannah for not telling me the truth about Myrtle, there was one thing I *did* know to be true.

Hannah would never have left me.

I sat there, biting my lip. I don't know how long I would have stayed there, or what decision I would have come to, if I hadn't heard a muffled *boom* in the distance.

Thunder? I thought. No, there wasn't a cloud in the sky. Besides, the sound had come from the direction of town.

Fireworks? No, they weren't till this evening.

But then I knew.

Dynamite.

The Wright brothers must have blown the dam after all.

All the stories I'd heard of Runaway Pond flooded into my brain. The water had washed away the mill, even carrying off the heavy millstone, which was never found. All through the valley, buildings were torn off their foundations, trees uprooted, animals carried away. The only reason there hadn't been more damage and deaths was because so little of the valley had been settled back then. That wasn't true now. How much of the town would be washed away this time? How many of the people?

People like me. All that water would be coming down the river, headed for me, any second now.

Dolly and I would be like a tiny speck of dust swept away without a trace by that wall of water.

I had to get to high ground fast. I kicked Dolly hard. She laid her ears back, but I think she sensed something and jogged along faster than usual. A little ways ahead, on the left, was a hill.

If we got to the top of the hill, we'd be all right there, I thought. We just had to get away from the river.

Then I remembered. Raleigh's animals were all along the river.

Raleigh was at the sesquicentennial, right this very minute, playing Spencer Chamberlain! But it was his animals here that were in the path of a *real* flood.

I raced across the bridge, not giving Dolly time to remember how she hated bridges. I kept glancing over my shoulder. How fast did water travel? If I'd studied harder in science, I'd know that.

I wondered what it must have been like for Spencer to be running with that roaring wall of water right behind him.

I raced to open gates and cages and fences. The heron hopped out, one wing flapping, the three heron babies hopping after her, and the monkey climbed the nearest tree. The other animals sensed something was up, and the sounds of bleating, bawling, baaing, and clucking drowned out any sound of approaching water. I carried, pushed, and prodded the sheep, calf, rabbit, chickens, and Daisy all to higher ground, until the only animal left was the camel.

It was then I heard the water coming, and it sounded like a train.

I grabbed the camel's halter, and what'd he do but lie down! I tugged and pulled, and even said some bad words, but that camel refused to budge. Didn't he know I was only trying to save him? Then I knew I was too late to do it. I let go of his halter and ran for Dolly.

As soon as I dropped the halter, that camel got up and loped off across the bridge. If I'd had any more time, I might have said a few more bad words, but I didn't. I took a running jump, vaulted onto Dolly's back, just like Tom Mix in the movies, and dug in my heels.

We were halfway across the bridge when Dolly balked— what was it with these fool animals? I jabbed my heels into her again and thought, We're going to beat it, we're going to get across in time, when the water slammed into us.

The next thing I knew, we were in the river, being tumbled like clothes in the wringer washing machine.

Water filled my ears, nose, and eyes. The last image I had of Dolly was of her flailing at the water with her hooves, and then I was churned underwater. When I popped back up, she was gone. Then the river pushed me under again.

What was that word that meant "pertaining to rivers"? *Flum . . . fluminous*, that was it. I was going to die a fluminous death.

I don't know how long I churned and tumbled down that river—minutes, hours, days?—before I felt a blinding pain in the side of my head, and suddenly I'm six years old again, and Hannah is teaching me how to do the dog paddle and back float in Shadow Lake. I'm afraid, but she tells me to trust her, to lean back on her hand and let the water hold me. I feel myself floating, and then, just as suddenly, I'm ten, and Hannah and I are paddling a canoe down the river. I turn my head to say something to Hannah, and I see a woman standing at the water's edge. The sun is shining like gold on her hair, and she's smiling, holding a hand out to me, and I know it's my mama. I try to paddle closer to her, but the river carries the canoe past her.

"Blue?" I can hear my mama calling me.

I'm coming, Mama, I tell her. I'm coming.

"Blue."

I opened my eyes.

Hannah's worried face stared back at me.

It took me a moment to realize I was sitting in the bathtub, neck-deep in warm water.

"It was the best way to warm you," Hannah said. "You're too big to fit in the oven now."

chapter 32

Behind Hannah, I could see the worried faces of all the quilting ladies and their husbands, Mr. Gilpin, and even Mr. Hazelton, all of them crowded into our little bathroom. I sank deeper into the water, hoping there were enough soapsuds to cover me up.

"Thank the Lord you've come back to us," said Mrs. Potter. "We were worried sick."

"Now, Hortense, don't be jumping on the girl," Mr. Potter said. "Just be glad she's all right."

"Of course I'm glad she's all right," Mrs. Potter said. "Can't you see I'm glad?" And she burst into tears. Mr. Potter patted her on the back. I could see tears in his eyes, too.

Were they crying over *me*?

"Thank goodness Hannah and Raleigh were out looking for you," Esther said.

I tried to follow what they were saying. Hannah and

Raleigh had been out looking for me? I'd thought they were at the pageant.

"Well, it was a good thing Clem happened to be fishing, too," Mr. Gilpin said. "He's the one that saved Dolly."

"I was coming from the creamery, headed to the celebration, when I saw the fish were jumping," Mr. Hazelton said. "You know, fish always bite better after a storm. So there I am fishing when I hear that water a'comin. Got to higher ground just in time. But when I saw poor ol' Dolly coming down the river, I took the rope holding the milk cans and lassoed her!"

Mr. Hazelton grinned.

"Biggest catch I ever pulled out of that river, I can tell you!" he said.

"The bravery of that young man, to jump in to save Blue," Mrs. Wells said. "How's he doing?"

I took it that she was talking about Raleigh, but none of this was making any sense. Raleigh was terrified of water. But he'd jumped in the river?

To rescue *me*.

"Doc says he's got a concussion and some water in the lungs," Mr. Gilpin said, "but he's going to be all right. Said he about had to tie Raleigh down to keep him from coming over here, he's that worried about you, Blue."

"We were *all* worried about you," Mrs. Fitch said. "We all care about you so much, Blue."

I could see a dozen heads bobbing vigorously.

"Without you, it'd be pretty dull around here," Mrs. Barclay said. "Us old folks need someone like you to liven things up."

More nods.

"And we're hoping you'll join the quilting group," Mrs. Thompson said. "I've got a good pattern for a beginner."

"Too bad we couldn't add *you* to the quilt," Mrs. Barclay said. "You and Raleigh are part of the town's history now."

"Gracious, yes," said Mrs. Potter. "It's a story they'll be telling around here for years."

"I think—" began Mrs. Gallagher, but Mr. Gilpin interrupted her.

"I think we need to give this girl some privacy, now that we know she's all right," he said. He herded everyone toward the door, except for one person I hadn't noticed until now.

Nadine.

"I thought you'd already left," I said.

"I had to make sure you were all right," Nadine said. "You're my best friend, you know." I don't know why that made the back of my throat ache, but it did.

"Are your folks still going to sell the camp?" I asked.

Nadine nodded. "But Mama says I can come visit you next summer. If that's okay with you."

I nodded right back at her. It was more than okay. She wasn't old Nadine or new Nadine anymore.

Just Nadine. My best friend, now and always.

"I wonder what will happen to the Wright brothers, causing such a stir," Hannah asked.

"Well, they hightailed it out of town," Mr. Gilpin said. "I imagine it's going to be some time before they dare show their faces around here again. They're lucky no one was killed, that explosion only punched a hole in the dam. If it'd blown the whole thing, well, that would be a different story. As it is, there are quite a few flooded buildings, including the *Monitor*."

"What a day," Hannah sighed. "Too bad about the celebration, Wallace. All that work you put into it, and now the whole thing will have to be cancelled."

"Who said anything like that?" Mr. Gilpin thundered. "I'm not cancelling the celebration. The history that I wrote washed away, but we're still putting on the pageant."

"You can use the history that Blue wrote," Nadine piped up.

I swiveled my head to look at her. How did she know about that? I wondered. I hadn't told Nadine I was doing it.

"I came by your house this morning to say goodbye," Nadine told me. "I went upstairs, looking for you, and that's when I found it."

Mr. Gilpin fixed his eyes on me.

"You didn't tell me you were writing a history," he said.

"It's j-just stories I wrote down that Hannah and the quilting ladies told," I stammered. "It's not very good."

"It is too!" Nadine almost shouted. "I wasn't supposed to read it, but I did, and it's really good."

"If Blue wrote it, I'm sure it is," Mr. Gilpin said. "I'm eager to read it. But right now I'm off to finish writing up this story before Roy scoops me, and get the paper out."

"But how?" Hannah asked. "The *Monitor*'s flooded."

"Roy says I can print the paper at his office till we can get everything dried out," Mr. Gilpin said. "I'm certain he won't mind if we print up Blue's history, too."

I was sure I hadn't heard right.

"Mr. Allard is going to let you print *there*?" I asked.

"Of course," Mr. Gilpin said, as if that were the most normal thing in the world. "I'd do the same for him."

"I did manage to rescue one thing from the office," Mr. Gilpin went on, and plopped his dictionary down on the chair beside the tub. "Thought you might be needing it."

I looked at him, not understanding.

"I'm offering you a job, after school and summers," Mr. Gilpin said. "That is, if you're planning on staying."

Hannah must have told him I'd run away, I thought. If so, he probably knew about the college fund jar too. I ducked my head in shame and gave a weak little nod.

"Good," Mr. Gilpin said. "Speaking of rescues—you were going to rescue his animals, weren't you?"

I wondered how he knew that, but I nodded again.

"That's what you were trying to tell me at Old Home

Day, wasn't it, about Raleigh's animals?" Mr. Gilpin said, as if reading my mind.

I looked at him in surprise, and he grinned.

"I'm not an investigative reporter for nothing, you know," he said. "Anyway, I want you to write up a story about Raleigh and how he's been rescuing and caring for those animals all these years, and we're going to see if we can't build him a wildlife sanctuary, where he can take care of birds and animals for as long as he wants to. I think it's his calling."

I thought so, too, and I thought how happy Raleigh would be that he could help even more animals.

"You'll be an apprentice, and work your way up, just like I did," Mr. Gilpin said. "That was a good piece of detective work you did, finding out about those missing animals, even if it did turn out to be Raleigh instead of the Wright brothers. Shows you've got the makings of a good reporter. Might even be *your* calling."

Mr. Gilpin opened the door, but paused, his hand on the doorknob.

"Who knows," he said. "You might even take over the paper someday."

He gave a little smile and clicked the door shut behind him.

chapter 33

It seemed too quiet with just me and Hannah.

"I'm sorry about the college fund—" I began, but Hannah nearly smothered me in a hug.

"It doesn't matter," she said. "Oh, Blue, I could have lost *you*."

I knew she must have about a hundred questions for me, and I had some for her, too.

"How'd you know—" I began again, meaning to ask how she'd known where to look for me, but Hannah didn't let me finish.

"I just knew you were in trouble," she said.

Hannah didn't say another word as she toweled me off, wrapped a quilt around me, set me on the couch, and fixed me a cup of cocoa, with extra marshmallows. When she sat down next to me, I figured I was going to get the talking-to of my life.

"Now," she said, "why were you running away?"

"Is Myrtle my mother?" I asked her.

Only a flicker of surprise crossed Hannah's face. She sat for what seemed like a century before she answered.

"Yes," she said. "From the moment I saw you, I knew. You were the spitting image of her."

She looked at me.

"I imagine you'd like to see some pictures of her," she said.

There were pictures of Myrtle? How could I have lived in this house for ten and a half years and not known that? I nodded.

Hannah went into her bedroom and came back out a few minutes later with a worn photo album. She showed me photos of Myrtle as a baby, in first grade, riding Dolly, paddling a canoe. If I squinted, any of those photos could have been of me.

There was one of her crying.

"That was at Old Home Day, when a clown tried to give her a balloon," Hannah said. "Myrtle never did like clowns."

A shiver ran through me. If finding my mama was like piecing a quilt, another piece had just got sewn into place.

There were later photos of Myrtle, too, in high school. Hannah pointed to one of them.

"This is the last photo I have of her," she said. "It was taken a month before she left."

The picture was a little blurry, but it showed Myrtle

standing in front of the barn, her hands tucked into her coat pockets.

"I've studied that picture a thousand times," Hannah said, "trying to figure out how I missed all the signs that *she* was in trouble, too.

"I wanted her to go to college so bad, to have the opportunities that I'd missed out on, I never asked what *she* wanted," Hannah continued. "Then, when I found you, I thought, Here's my second chance."

I thought of the college fund jar, and felt my face flush with shame. All that hard-saved money lost, and Hannah's dreams dashed again.

I stared at Myrtle's face.

"What was she like?" I whispered.

"She was stubborn as a mule," Hannah said. "Whenever I told her to do something, she gave me eleven reasons why she shouldn't have to."

"She sounds obstreperous," I said without thinking. That had been one of the words I'd learned from "It Pays to Increase Your Word Power." That seemed a hundred years ago.

Hannah looked startled, then burst out laughing.

"Yes, obstreperous, but she had a sweet side, too. She was her father's daughter, through and through, and I guess I'm glad Herbert died before Myrtle ran away, because I'm sure that would have killed him. It pretty near killed me. I don't know what I would have done if you hadn't come into my life, Blue."

233

My throat closed up, and I was afraid I was going to start bawling. In all my ten years, I'd never heard Hannah say so much, or with so much feeling.

"Why did she leave?" I asked.

Hannah sighed.

"After Herbert died, I was grieving so much that I couldn't see how much Myrtle was grieving, too. I'm sure she just wanted to get away. She met a boy at a dance, and they started seeing each other. I didn't think she was old enough to be dating, and I didn't think this boy was good enough for her. He was wild, and reckless, and I thought he was going to break her heart, but part of it was selfish, too. I didn't want her leaving me to rattle around in this house all alone. So I put my foot down, forbade her to see him. She told me one night that he was coming for her, that they were going to run off together, but he didn't show up. Turned out, coming to get her, he crashed his car. They pulled him out alive, but Doc didn't give him much chance of surviving and said he'd have brain damage if he did. Next thing I knew, Myrtle had disappeared. Wasn't but a month later that you were left in my yard."

I closed my eyes. It was just too much to take in.

"It's true, that old saying, Be careful what you wish for, it might come true," Hannah said. "After Myrtle left, all I wanted was for her to come back. But then I was terrified she would."

I couldn't imagine Hannah terrified. Why wouldn't she want her daughter back? And wasn't that the same as Myrtle not wanting *me* back?

I kept my eyes closed, just letting Hannah talk.

"I was afraid she'd take you back, Blue," Hannah said. "It was almost as if I'd made a trade, Myrtle for you, and I wasn't willing to trade back."

That I could understand. It was what I'd been wrestling with, out there, before I got hit by the water, deciding if I was willing to trade Hannah for Myrtle.

"I'm sorry, Blue," Hannah said. "I wanted to do better by you, but it looks like I've just made the same mistakes. I should have told you about Myrtle, and I should have told you more often how proud I am of you."

Well, I hadn't done a very good job letting Hannah know how I felt about her, either.

"You were foolish risking your life to rescue those animals," Hannah went on. "But very brave, too. But then I guess you would be, being Spencer Chamberlain's great-great-great-great-granddaughter."

I opened my eyes and stared into Hannah's face, not understanding.

"The boy Myrtle loved," Hannah said. "It was Raleigh."

Raleigh? Raleigh True?

My *father*?

"When I heard him call you Blue True, I knew for certain that Myrtle must have told him she was going to have a baby, that's why they were going to run off together," Hannah said.

I thought of the initials carved in the rock: M + R.

Myrtle and Raleigh.

Hannah sighed.

"I just wish she'd been able to tell me," she said.

All this time, I'd been wondering about and looking for my *mother,* and my *father* had been right here, the whole time.

All this time, Raleigh had been trying to tell me.

Only four words, but they told my story: *Blue True, baby, Myrtle.* The clues had been there all along, if only I'd listened.

Raleigh True.

My father.

Hannah stood up and rummaged around in the desk drawer. She handed me a piece of paper. Myrtle's name was on it, and an address out in California.

"It's an old address, so she might have moved," Hannah said. "She never answered any of my letters. But she just might answer one from you."

Finally, after all this searching, was I going to find my real mama?

Hannah reached for her sweater.

"I hate leaving you home alone," she said, "but Mabel's mother is doing poorly. They think she may pass tonight. I thought I'd go sit with her, if you think you're all right."

That was Hannah. Not only did she help the living, but she helped ease their passing on into the next life, too.

Hannah picked up her bag and headed for the door.

"Did you see Cat today?" I asked.

Hannah gave a little shake of her head and left.

The room seemed as big as a barn, the only sounds the hiss of the fire in the stove and the soft ticking of the clock. It had been just a few hours since I'd left this morning.

It seemed like a million years.

I pulled the quilt around me and sat by the stove trying to sort out how I felt. Melancholy? Forlorn? Atrabilarious? But I was tired of all the big words.

I just felt plain blue.

Maybe that's why Hannah had named me Blue. Maybe that's how she'd felt, with a daughter who had just run off. Maybe Blue was the only name that seemed right.

I thought about Raleigh and Myrtle, and how their dreams of a life together had shattered. I could see why Myrtle had run off, but why hadn't she ever come back for me?

I even thought about Cat. I'd loved her, but she'd left me, too. My own mama hadn't wanted me, and now Cat hadn't wanted me, either.

With so many thoughts tumbling through my head, I was sure I wouldn't be able to sleep a wink, but no one had told that to my eyelids, so I was sinking into sleep when a floorboard on the porch creaked.

chapter 34

I froze as whatever it was shuffled across the porch. I thought of the ghost stories that Keith had told me and Nadine.

The hair rose prickly on my neck.

Something bumped against the door. I burrowed down into the couch, wishing I could hide under it.

Something, or *someone*, was outside.

What if it was Myrtle, come back for me, I wondered.

What if it wasn't?

I was off the couch in an instant and snatched up Hannah's rolling pin. Holding it over my head, I reached for the doorknob. What if the man with the hook was on the other side, reaching for the doorknob right now . . . ?

I shuddered and cracked open the door.

Cat stood on the porch.

I held my breath, afraid if I blinked, Cat would disappear

and it would be just a dream, but last I'd heard, dreams don't step into a kitchen and rub up against your leg.

I reached down slowly and Cat let me pick her up, but she gave a little cry and I saw why. Her right front leg was swollen to three times its normal size.

"Oh, Cat," I said, softly. "What happened to you?"

Cat tucked her head under my arm. She was hot with fever, and I could feel her pounding heart.

My own heart was pounding, too. After all these weeks, I couldn't believe I was holding her.

I sat by the fire, holding Cat as gently as I could, and scratched under her chin. I wished Hannah were home; she'd know how to doctor Cat. Because we didn't have a telephone, I couldn't call her or Dr. Todd, the veterinarian, and I didn't know what else to do, so I simply sat and patted Cat. She even purred a little, sick as she was.

Cat made up her own mind when it was time to leave. I'd been hoping she'd stay the night where we could keep an eye on her, and I didn't want to let her go, but she struggled and I was afraid of hurting her leg, so I set her on the floor. Cat limped to the door and stood there, waiting.

"Don't go, Cat," I said. But Cat stood, her nose against the door, and I knew I had to let her go. I could hardly bear to watch her hobble away.

I washed the dishes and was sweeping when I heard the bump again. I ran to open the door.

Cat held a small kitten in her mouth.

I knelt on the floor and Cat placed the kitten in my hands. I closed my eyes and held the kitten under my chin.

"Oh, Cat, he's so soft," I said, but when I opened my eyes, Cat was gone.

I stepped onto the porch.

"Cat!" I called out into the night, and I was still standing there, holding the kitten, when Hannah came home.

Hannah heated milk in a saucepan and showed me how to feed the kitten with an eyedropper. I told her of Cat's swollen leg.

"Cat knew she couldn't take care of her kitten anymore," Hannah said. "She brought it to someone she knew would," and looking into Hannah's warm, gentle face, I wondered if my mama had left me here with Hannah for that very same reason.

chapter 35

A few days later, I found Cat's body, and I buried her in the orchard. I buried the quilt with her. I'm not looking for my mama anymore. Who left me isn't as important as who rescued me, and even if my own mama were to knock on our door tomorrow and want to take me with her, I guess I'd stay right here. Hannah might be my grandma, but she's the only *mama* I've ever known.

"One person's trash is another person's treasure," I've heard Hannah say, and it's true. Someone threw Cat away but I loved her, and I know Hannah treasures me. We might not have much on this tumbledown farm, but we've got everything we need.

Raleigh's living with us now. Hannah said he might as well, seeing as he's family. The flood washed away his whole house, and I felt bad, at first, that he lost everything saving me, but Hannah said, "That's just *stuff*, Blue. Doesn't hold a candle to a *daughter*," and I see it's true. Whenever I call Raleigh Daddy, his face lights up like a lantern.

I talk to Cat as I plant tulip bulbs on her grave.

"Don't you worry, Cat," I tell her. "I'm taking good care of your kitten." Spencer's getting bigger every day, and it makes me laugh to watch him chasing leaves.

"Blue," Hannah calls. I see her in the doorway, eyes shaded, searching for me, and Raleigh's already in the truck. We're going into town to see the movie *The African Queen*, and Hannah doesn't want to be late.

"Coming, Mama," I answer. I pick up Spencer and run for home.

One thing I've learned this summer is that the *smallest* words are the most powerful, like *home* and *mama*.

And *love*.

acknowledgments

I want to thank, from the bottom of my heart, my family and dear friends. Seven years ago, my sister, an uncle, and a cousin died within six months of each other, and my writing voice died with them. Only with the love and support of family and friends were we able to get through that difficult time. With their help, my writing voice returned and I'm grateful to be back doing what I love, writing family stories. Genealogy was my sister's passion, and I try to ignite that same passion for history and family stories in children and adults everywhere.

I want to give a special thank-you to my editor, Nancy Hinkel, who kept believing in me through those years, and whose unwavering support and encouragement made this a better book than it would have been otherwise. I hope the wait was worth it.

about the author

Natalie Kinsey-Warnock grew up on a dairy farm in the Northeast Kingdom of Vermont, where her Scottish ancestors settled in the early 1800s. She still lives there, with her husband, Tom, and the many horses, dogs, and cats she has rescued. Natalie has written several other books, most of them based on her childhood, her ancestors, and her true family stories, and she encourages students everywhere to look for *their* family stories. Her first book for Knopf was the acclaimed historical novel *Gifts from the Sea*.

Natalie is an athlete, naturalist, writer, historian, and artist, and her hobbies include biking, kayaking, cross-country skiing, hiking, bagpiping, fiddling, Civil War history, bird carving, quilting, and genealogy. She is developing a new history curriculum for schools, based on students researching their own family genealogy and history. You can learn more about Natalie by visiting her website, kinsey-warnock.com.